William thought about the Patrol as he put one foot in front of the other, and Suzy and Mulberry walked beside him matching their strides to his. How long would it last? he wondered. He had thought their fight against fire had been hard, but this was worse. This was a fight against life and death, he thought, because if we don't reach the cattle truck soon, we'll be lost, walking in circles, and no one will ever find us.

Also by Christine Pullein-Thompson:

Pony Patrol

Christine Pullein-Thompson

PONY PATROL S.O.S.

Illustrated by Jennifer Bell

SIMON & SCHUSTER

LONDON • SYDNEY • NEW YORK • TOKYO • SINGAPORE • TORONTO

Cover photograph taken at Poynters Riding Centre,
Ockham Lane, Cobham, Surrey.

First published in Great Britain in 1991
by Simon and Schuster Young Books

Photoset in North Wales by
Derek Doyle & Associates, Mold, Clwyd.
Printed and bound in Great Britain at
The Guernsey Press

Simon and Schuster Young Books
Simon and Schuster Ltd
Wolsey House
Wolsey Road
Hemel Hempstead HP2 4SS

British Library Cataloguing in Publication Data
Pullein-Thompson, Christine
Pony Patrol S.O.S.
I. Title II. Series
823.914 [F]

ISBN 0 7500 0807 5
ISBN 0 7500 0808 3 (pbk)

Contents

Chapter One

Loading up

Amanda's mother was clucking like a broody hen, her eyes still puffy with sleep.

"I'll take you to William's place in the car," she said. "I can't have you going on a bike in this weather."

They could hear the rain falling outside. Amanda found a waterproof; it was short and blue and wouldn't cover her knees when she was riding.

"Have you put on plenty of clothes underneath? It will be cold on the marshes," her mother said.

Amanda nodded. "If I start to freeze, I'll get off and run," she answered. She was broad shouldered, calm and capable. She put a packet of sandwiches in her pocket, string, and a pocket knife. It was two-forty a.m. as she followed her mother outside. It was still dark and there was no sound but the falling rain.

"Have you got 20p for a phone call?" asked her mother, opening the garage doors.

"Oh, Mum, do stop fussing," said Amanda. "William will be there and Marvin, *and* the police. Whatever can happen to me? You're mad."

Her father tapped on a window calling goodbye.

He was wearing pyjamas and his grey hair was on end. Amanda waved back thinking, it will be light when we get there, dawn. She pictured a group of riders gathered together, the police with dogs, even the Army perhaps, all looking for one small mentally retarded girl, who had wandered off yesterday afternoon probably clutching a teddy bear.

Amanda had looked at the map the night before, after William and other members of the Pony Patrol had left. She knew now that beyond the marshes lay the sea. The Patrol had nearly come to an end the night before but had decided to continue on to search for the little girl. It was made up of riders ready to take part in any emergency, and to fight for what was right. William Gaze was its leader.

"Are you riding Suzy?" asked her mother starting the car.

"Yes, but I wish it was my own Tango," replied Amanda.

"You'll never see her again. She wasn't the only horse stolen last year. And none of them have been found. You really must forget her, darling," her mother answered.

"She was so wonderful, the best horse ever," said Amanda sadly.

"When things get better, we'll buy you another one. That's a promise," her mother said.

They could see the lights of the farmhouse now, shining across the valley. The yard light was on too. It looked as though no one had slept all night.

"I hope William put Suzy in before he went to bed, otherwise she'll be soaking wet," said Amanda.

"You are fond of William aren't you?" asked her mother, with a sigh.

"Yes. He's the nicest person I know. He's lent me Suzy time and time again, and he's incredibly brave," replied Amanda. She could see the Gaze's cattle truck now, ready with the ramp down and William crossing the yard with a brush in his hand. He was tall and thin, but strong too, the sort of person who never gives up. It was nearly three a.m. now and they were leaving at three fifteen, because it was forty kilometres to the marshes, and they had to pick up another two horses on the way.

Amanda leapt out of the car shouting, "I'll groom Suzy! Bye Mum. See you later." She could hear a cow lowing in the byres and a dog rushed forward to lick her hand.

William had hardly slept all night, afraid he might not hear the alarm clock ringing, because he was exhausted already.

He had dark hair, blue eyes, a straight nose and a mouth which rarely smiled, but when it did, transformed his whole face. He wasn't hard – he loved his horses more than anything else on earth – but he was tough and determined. Rain didn't matter to him, storms didn't scare him; he could lift a sack of oats without effort and change a Landrover wheel in less than five minutes.

His horse, Boxer, was lame, so he was taking his father's hunter to the marshes. He was a large, roan gelding called Mulberry, with a roman nose and hoofs like soup plates. He was patient and well behaved and kind, but he wasn't fast and couldn't jump like Boxer. He was lending Amanda his Prince Philip Competition pony, Suzy, who was quick and fast and not traffic shy. He had caught them both the night before and put them in warm boxes bedded down with shavings. He had risen at two a.m. to give them feeds and there were hay-nets waiting for them in the cattle truck.

William was wearing an old-fashioned riding waterproof, a riding hat, breeches and rubber boots. His mother had risen to cook him a breakfast of bacon and eggs, which he could hardly eat. She had made him ham sandwiches, packed a basket of food and drink and put it in the cab of the cattle truck. She was always fussing over food. "A car can't run without petrol in its tank, and a person can't work without food inside him," she was always saying.

William's father had put petrol in the cattle truck. He might have been riding himself if he hadn't arthritis. He greeted Amanda warmly calling out, "How are you, gal? Ready are you?"

They stored the tack in the cattle truck and fetched the horses.

"What a night for a little girl to be out on the marshes," William said.

"I'm frightened she won't have survived," replied Amanda.

"No, she'll have crawled in somewhere, you'll see," answered William, sounding like his father.

Suzy and Mulberry boxed without trouble and they could hear a cock crowing in the chicken house.

"It's the lights. He thinks it's dawn," explained William. He liked Amanda. She wasn't too smart, or what he called 'toffee nosed', and she rode beautifully, better than him, he often thought. Mr Gaze threw up the ramp. They climbed into the cab.

Mrs Gaze called, "Good luck. You find the little

mite and don't come home until you have —"

"Don't listen to her. She doesn't know anything about it," said Mr Gaze, starting the engine.

"I wish it would stop raining," announced Amanda. "It's going to be horribly wet on the marshes."

Marvin was peeling off chestnut Skinflint's bandages. He had overslept and had been awakened by his mother rushing into his room at three a.m. calling, "Marvin, get up at once! You're late! It's gone three and the Gazes are picking you up at half past."

There wasn't time for breakfast. Marvin put his pullover on inside out and odd socks on his feet.

"You're hopeless," his mother said. "Absolutely impossible and totally unreliable." She was large and strong and could ride herself. Marvin's stable management never reached her high standard, however hard he tried. His tack was never cleaned well enough, and Skinflint's box always had droppings under the straw.

"I can't help you because I've got a migraine," she said now.

"A migraine?" asked Marvin, rubbing sleep from his eyes.

"A headache," she said. "My temples are throbbing."

"It doesn't matter, I can manage," Marvin said.

Skinflint was lying down when he reached the loosebox. He blinked when Marvin switched on the electric light. He looked sweet and cuddly, like a toy horse. Marvin tipped a feed into his manger. Damn the rain, he thought. I hate getting wet. And I haven't any leather gloves and my string ones will be soaked in five minutes. Why did I say I would go? The police will be looking for her anyway. He felt very weak and still half asleep. I hope the others will have brought something to eat, he thought. I'm starving. He could hear the cattle truck coming now and Skinflint was still eating his feed, and he couldn't undo the knots on the bandages. I wish I was still in bed, he thought. I've had enough of early mornings. If only Mum would let me, I'd sleep till lunchtime every day. I hate getting up.

"He won't be ready," William said, as the cattle truck turned into the small concrete yard near the done-up Tudor cottage where Marvin lived. "What did I say? He hasn't even got the bandages off yet."

"I'll help," replied Amanda jumping out of the cab. There were no lights on in the cottage and it looked small and dreamy in the lights from the truck.

"I'm sorry. I overslept. I didn't hear the clock. I was too tired. I haven't even had breakfast," shouted Marvin.

"It's all right, we're three minutes early and there's plenty of food in the cattle truck. You know what Mrs Gaze is like. You can hardly move for it. Great thermoses of coffee and tea, fruit cake, chicken pâté, sandwiches galore . . . " Amanda said, undoing the last bandage, running to the saddle room for the tack, while Marvin led Skinflint into the pouring rain.

"I've forgotten any hay," he said.

"It's all right, there's some in the truck. Load up for goodness' sake," replied William, looking at his watch. He was tense now for he hated being late.

Skinflint could have gone in his own trailer if Marvin's parents had wanted to help, but of course they didn't! They were quite happy for William's father to do the work, while they stayed in bed, warm and dry. Ignorant townies, thought William angrily, throwing up the ramp behind Skinflint.

"We've one more horse to collect. A stranger called Alison Carruthers is coming. I don't know who she is. She telephoned last night and begged a lift. Her horse is called Rainbow," he said.

"Let's hope he improves the weather then," answered Mr Gaze, laughing.

"Who else is coming?" asked Marvin.

"No one local as far as I know. They didn't want anyone under thirteen, so that ruled out quite a lot of people," answered William. "But there's an old chap organizing the horses, so there will be lots of other people as well as us, so don't worry."

"I'm not," replied Marvin, "but can I have something to eat? We only had tomatoes on toast for supper last night, and I'm starving."

Alison Carruthers was tall and fair and always well turned-out. Her hair never moved out of place and her buttons were always on her coat, and she never lost anything. She was waiting for the trailer, standing at some crossroads in the pouring rain with Rainbow, who was golden dun with a crooked streak of white running down his face. He was wearing a waterproof rug and Alison was wearing a waterproof too, turned up over her neck.

"This *is* kind of you," she called. "I'm so grateful. I couldn't get a box. No one wanted to collect us at three a.m. and, anyway, I only had twelve hours' notice, and really that isn't long enough to arrange anything."

"It's a pleasure," replied Mr Gaze, getting out of the cab.

"I'll ride in the truck," said Alison. "I don't mind, honestly. I always do."

"I'll travel with you, then," offered Amanda.

"That is nice of you," replied Alison, "but you don't have to."

"I want to," replied Amanda. "There's an empty space in the front. We can get up through the little door."

Soon they were on their way again, the horses travelling peacefully, munching hay, Amanda and Alison talking, liking each other instantly, while in the cab Marvin ate as though he hadn't eaten for weeks. And none of them had any idea of what awaited them, of the disasters which were to befall them, of the mess and the muddle and the despair.

Chapter Two

The search

They were the first to arrive at the old army bunker at the end of a rough lane, which was the rendezvous. They stood drinking coffee, listening to the pitiful cry of gulls, as dawn came slowly. It was very cold. A freezing wind loaded with salt from the sea whipped their faces. It was too cold to unbox the horses, too cold for anything but standing hunched with your back to the wind and the rain.

"Where did she wander from?" asked Alison, after a time.

"I don't know. The police rang up. We've been running a patrol to catch the arsonists who were setting fire to farmers' haystacks and they knew about us," William replied.

"Our Pony Club commissioner rang me," Alison said.

They could see headlights now, bumping along the rough lane.

"Shall we unbox?" asked Alison.

"Not yet," answered Mr Gaze. "We don't want the horses wet before they have to be."

"If only the sun would come out," moaned Marvin.

A Range Rover followed the horse box. When it stopped, a large tweedy-looking man stepped out, in green boots, waterproof suit and a deer-stalker.

"The name's Metcalf," he said, holding out his hand to Mr Gaze. "I'm in charge. The mounted search was my idea. We are taking the north side. The little girl is probably three kilometres south of here, but the police couldn't cover the whole area, and there aren't any Army chaps available, though they may send in a helicopter later, so I said I would run a mounted unit. We're on our own, if you know what I mean. There's no support unit to back us up."

"When do we start?" asked William.

"In ten minutes," replied Mr Metcalf.

They started to unbox, while Mr Metcalf continued talking: "Search any drains, stacks of hay or straw, anywhere where she could have crawled in to get out of the rain. Look in ditches, sluices, anywhere she might have drowned. Ask people. Don't be shy. Search all sheds, outbuildings. Who's the leader?" he asked.

"I am," said William, stepping forward.

"Good. You're responsible for your group then. How many are there in it?"

"Only four."

"Fine. Here's a whistle for each of you, long piercing notes mean you've found something. Like this . . . " Mr Metcalf blew loud and long, making the gulls shriek and the horses leap sideways. "Short blasts to keep in touch with each other."

"When do we turn back?" William wanted to know.

"When you reach the sea."

"How far is that?"

"Not more than ten miles straight as a die. I've got maps of the area for all of you. Here, hand them out with the whistles." Mr Metcalf was moving on now to another group of riders that had just arrived.

"I'm scared," Amanda said.

"Same here," agreed Alison.

"We don't know what she's like. Ask him, William, if he knows."

"You ask him yourself."

Mulberry was tacked up now, ready. The mud was deep and heavy and it was still raining.

"I'll be back here by noon, waiting," said Mr Gaze. "Watch your step, the sea can be a bit wild at this time of year."

"We're not going swimming," snapped William.

He was on edge now; the landscape in front of him stretched for miles, dark and pitiless. The wind beat his face, making his eyes run. He wished he had come alone because, suddenly, he didn't want the responsibility of the others.

Amanda was talking to Mr Metcalf now, getting more instructions. "What's the little girl like?" she asked at last. He pulled a photograph from his pocket and they passed it round. The girl looked at least nine years old with short hair, and eyes which seemed to be looking beyond them into space. "She's wearing a dress, white ankle socks – though I don't suppose they are white any more – sandals, a cardigan. Nothing else . . . " explained Mr Metcalf.

"She'll be frozen stiff then," Marvin said, shivering.

They were mounting now. William recieved last-minute instructions before they took up position, with ten metres between each of them.

"You'll have to use your own initiative," Mr

Metcalf said to William. "But never lose sight of the person on your right; that's the golden rule. But you are experienced, aren't you? I've heard of your exploits, read about you in the paper."

"I've never done anything like this before," replied William.

"And be back here by noon without fail, because fog is forecast later and if you are lost in that, God help you," said Mr Metcalf.

William chose the middle postion with the two girls on his left because they wanted to stay together, and Marvin on his right. His body was shaking with cold already, his nose dripping. The other riders were moving nearer to the police, whom they could hear faintly in the distance. The clouds were lifting, and they could see the landscape properly now – sagging wire fences, dykes, farms in the distance, rain, mud, wet cows, a heap of old machinery.

"Check watches, synchronize time. It's six a.m. Be back here by noon; one p.m. at the latest. Off you go, then," said Mr Metcalf, raising his arm.

"Good luck," said Mr Gaze.

Amanda and Alison were talking already.

"Stop nattering," yelled William. "This isn't a party. We're looking for a little girl."

"She can't be here. We would all have seen her if she was," retorted Amanda.

"How do you know?" asked William.

"Don't ask silly questions," said Amanda.

The horses were cold; they jogged and snatched at their bits. Marvin kept thinking of his bed at home, of how he might have been lying there still sound asleep. I hate charity work, he thought angrily.

"Does the little girl talk, William?" yelled Alison.

"How would I know?"

"He's cute, isn't he, really gorgeous," Alison said to Amanda. "Have you known him long?"

"Years and years, or so it seems. He's got the most fabulous farm, really old-fashioned, if you know what I mean. Going there is like putting the clock back fifty years. It's heavenly," Amanda answered.

"Why haven't we met before?" asked Alison. "You and me, I mean."

"Stop talking and look," yelled William.

The rain was beginning to lift; it was only a drizzle now which stung his face as he stared into the distance, looking for a crevice, for a hillock, for anything a little girl might shelter behind.

"I do a lot with the Pony Club," Alison said.

"But it's not the same as ours, or we would have met."

"Yes, but let's meet now we know each other."

"You must join the Patrol. We need new members," Amanda answered. "It hasn't been formed long. You have to swear an oath of allegiance."

"I will. I shall love it," cried Alison. "You all seem so nice. My mother's a bit odd, but you won't mind that, will you?"

"Mine is, too. She's terribly fussy, if you know what I mean."

"Stop talking. Look," yelled William.

"We'd better separate. We are not supposed to ride together. See you later," Amanda said. Suzy jogged and went sideways. Amanda thought of home, of her father getting up for the second time, of the newspaper coming through the letter box, of boiled eggs in wooden egg cups on the breakfast table. The rain was stopping at last, and it was really daylight now, and you could almost smell the sea.

William saw nothing but flat fields with an occasional tree withered and bent towards him by the constant wind from the sea. The trees made him think of old men twisted with rheumatism, and he thought, it will be easier riding back because the wind will be behind us then. Mulberry plodded on. His dam had been a Clydesdale and he had the same plod as a horse pulling a plough, steady, tireless, as relentless as the landscape.

Skinflint hated the wind. He didn't want to go into it. He flinched at every stinging drop of rain. Like Marvin, he wanted to be at home, munching hay, warm and comfortable. Marvin imagined his father reading the share prices in the morning newspaper before he set off for work, a tired educated man wearing gold-rimmed glasses. Marvin wanted to be like him one day, as quiet and self-contained. He never does anything for anyone else, so why should I? He thought now. Why am I here? I must be mad!

Alison's father had walked out of the house two days after she was born. Her mother had supported and brought up Alison and her three brothers ever since. Life had been hard, and the hardness showed on her mother's face. Alison had learned to sew on buttons early in life, to cook, and to keep her bedroom ship-shape. She looked after Rainbow entirely herself. She intended going up in the world. If she couldn't be a dentist, she intended being a show jumper.

The rain stopped completely and the sky cleared,

and the flat, windswept countryside had a dark sombre beauty of its own. They could see other riders now in the distance, and, beyond them, tiny figures who could be the police. William started to trot. Ahead lay a farm which must be searched, every building, even the house itself, because the girl might be inside. He wished he was older, taller, with a louder voice. He turned to yell to the others, "Meet you at the farm."

Then Alison blew her whistle three times. "There's something here, down a drain," she yelled.

They swung their horses towards her with one accord. Supposing she's dead, thought Amanda with panic, what shall we do then?

Alison was shivering. "Look, it's in a sack," she yelled.

William dismounted. "Someone take my horse," he said. The 'something' was a sack in an open drain through which water ran in a dark, evil-smelling trickle.

"It looks rather small," he said. He got down on his knees and took hold of the sack.

"How can you?" cried Amanda.

"Can't you ever shut up, even for a minute?" demanded Marvin.

The water seeped down William's sleeve. He pulled up the sack. "It's a dead cat," he said after a moment. "Come on, remount."

"Sorry," said Alison.

"There's bound to be false alarms," replied William.

"Better to be safe than sorry," said Amanda.

"See you at the farm," said William.

There was a helicopter in the sky now, flying

low. It made Marvin feel safer. If anything goes wrong, it can pick us up, he thought.

A track led to the farm. The lights were on in the house. There were sacks of newly lifted potatoes in the barn and an overpowering smell of sugar beet. Amanda and Marvin held the horses while the others searched. Alison wanted to talk to William, but he looked aloof and unapproachable. He walked round the sacks of potatoes, kicking them with his feet, and pointing to another building, said "You search that one. And look everywhere – in every nook and cranny. This is just the sort of place she could be sheltering in."

There was a barn full of straw. He went over it inch by inch, thinking, we'll be here for ever, but we can't afford to miss anything. I wish I'd brought one of the dogs with me, he thought a moment later as a rat ran past and he heard mice squeaking.

He walked towards the house and a man came out calling, "She ain't here. You go somewhere else. I've searched the place. You're wasting you time."

"You know about her, then?" William asked.

"Of course I do. It was on the radio, six o'clock this morning. I went straight out and looked, took the dogs too."

"Thank you very much," William said.

He found Alison searching pig sties. "She isn't here. The farmer's searched already," he said.

They mounted their horses and went on. They could here the distant roar of the sea now and the smell was stronger. It was eight a.m. They stopped again to search a ditch, a horse shelter, some straw stacked under a tarpaulin in a field. The sky was darker now and the horses were becoming bored.

Mulberry kept suggesting going back, and Suzy tried to swing round at every opportunity, while Rainbow walked slower and slower; and Skinflint threw his head about and jogged, pretending to see ghosts behind every lump of earth or piece of hedgerow.

"Keep looking," yelled William. He was finding it difficult to keep his eyes open now. They seemed to have been riding for hours already, and the howling wind made his head ache.

Then Amanda yelled, "There's a shack ahead and horses. Shall we meet there?" Staring ahead, William saw it, low lying, sheltered by trees, a mile or more away.

"Okay," he shouted, "but go on looking." He halted Mulberry and stared over a hedge. He stopped to look down a rabbit hole, even to search under an old wagon. All the time he could feel time passing, and he thought, we must be getting near the sea at last; we can gallop back to make up lost time; as long as we start back by eleven thirty, we must be all right.

There were no more roads or lanes now. Even the electricity wires had stopped. But there were ditches everywhere with water trickling throught them to the sea. He had fallen behind the others and was riding across ploughed fields where cabbages grew in their thousands. Mulberry's hoofs left huge dents in the soil and sliced whole cabbages in half. He could hear the others talking, shouting to on another, laughing. He pushed Mulberry into a trot, yelling, "Look, will you! This isn't a tea party."

Fifty metres away, Marvin thought, there's William

throwing his weight about again. Who does he think he is? Anyway the child may be found already. We're just wasting time here. Why weren't we given walkie-talkie sets? This whole expedition is really disorganized. I thought the police would be in charge. And where is the Army? Skinflint was covered with mud; his beautiful saddle was soaked with rain, his bridle would be like cardboard tomorrow when it was dry, and Marvin's mother would go on and on about it. Why did you stay out so long? Why didn't you turn back earlier? Just look at your tack. You know your saddle cost three hundred pounds, don't you? she would say, and Skinflint would be dirty too. He would have to be washed all over in a speical shampoo. Marvin's mother would go on and on about mud fever and how he never bothered about anyone but himself. She always blames me for everything, he thought. I wish I could go to boarding school. I might get some peace there.

Amanda and Alison were trotting now and shrieking to each other about everything under the sun, about pop groups, horses, boys, clothes, about their boring parents who never understood anything.

"I want to be a vet when I'm grown up," yelled Amanda. "The training lasts for ever and I've got to do loads of exams."

"I want to be a dentist," yelled back Alison.

The trees sheltering the shack were bare of leaves, though it was only October. They looked whipped to death by the wind from the sea. The whole place appeared deserted, except for the horses which stood thin and clear-cut against the horizon. Their fields were fenced by sagging wire, the posts chewed nearly through by horses' teeth. There were chickens scratching by the shack, and smoke coming from a chimney in a thin grey-black spiral. Then a dog started barking, followed by another and another, until there was a great crescendo of barking, which completely drowned the distant roaring of the sea.

"I don't think a little girl would have dared to shelter here," shouted Alison.

"She could be deaf. We must look just the same," yelled Amanda. They were all trotting now; the barking was growing louder each moment, and the horses were reluctant to go forward, sensing enemies at every stride.

"Go on, you old fool," shouted William to Mulberry.

"It's all right, darling," said Alison to Rainbow.

"It sounds like a pack of hounds," shouted Amanda.

"Wrong sort of bark," replied Alison.

They had drifted closer and closer until now they were riding side by side again.

"It's exciting, isn't it?" cried Amanda, "If only the weather would change.'

William was cantering, while Marvin was fighting Skinflint who wanted to go home. "After this, we'll go back," he said, hitting Skinflint with the end of his reins. "We won't listen to what William says. I bet the police have found the little girl hours ago anyway, and everybody else is home and dry by now."

It was now ten minutes to ten.

Chapter Three

Starving horses

The shack was made of wood and corrugated iron. It had been built onto several times; there were two doors and a multitude of windows, and at every window there seemed to be a cat looking out.

"Do you think it's a home for cats?" Alison asked.

"No, more likely it belongs to someone odd, to one of those old ladies who leave everything to a cats' home," replied Amanda.

The boys had nearly caught up with them now. The horses in the fields raised tired heads on the ends of pitifully thin necks and stared at them. Their backs stood up like precipices supporting ribs like toast racks. The fields had no grass left in them, just dark, wet mud and horse droppings.

It's like the end of the world, like hell, thought William, drawing rein. The trees were shrivelled and bent. Cats stared at them and spat, while a strange collection of dogs barked frantically against wire netting. There were spaniel-types, collies, a tiny terrier, a beagle, a solemn-faced long-eared basset hound, an arrogant alsatian, and a host of mongrels of all shapes and sizes.

"What a place!" gasped William.

"It's filthy. Disgusting. Whew! it stinks!" cried Marvin. "The child can't be here. Let's get on. It's getting late. You know what old Metcalf said about a fog. Look, it's ten o'clock."

"We must just knock at the door and ask," replied William, dismounting.

"There's no one about. I tell you it's empty."

"With all these animals about?" retorted William.

The place made Marvin feel ill. He had a dog at home, a neat well-groomed corgi, whose sire had been reserve champion at Crufts. He hated mongrels, and he found the cats loathsome too, for three had eyes missing and several had no tails, and the rest seemed to be expecting kittens. The few chickens looked diseased too; there were some with bloody wattles and other with no feathers, and a duck with only one leg.

"Let's go home and tell the R.S.P.C.A. about it," he suggested, without much hope.

"We are looking for a lost child – remember?" asked William, hitching Mulberry's reins over a convenient post. He walked up a crooked path surrounded by snarling, barking dogs. He walked backwards so that he could watch them, knowing that if he appeared to be retreating, they would attack. He refused to be frightened, because they would know at once by his smell and, again, launch an attack. He had to play it cool. There were flower pots all over the window ledges as well as cats. William turned a little to bang on the door and a terrier-type seized the opportunity to snap at his legs, and the cats inside arched their backs and spat at him through the cobwebbed window panes.

Amanda watched him reach the door in safety,

then turned to inspect the horses. They were a horrific sight, their skins sore with lice, starvation making them angular where they should be round, their foreheads appearing moth-eaten from constant rubbing to relieve the itching caused by lice and lack of vitamins. Their eyes were dull and lifeless. And yet, in spite of this, there was something familiar about one of them. Amanda couldn't decide what it was at first, then suddenly she knew – the best of the lot, the one with breeding and a beautifully cut head which no starvation could disguise, was her own long-lost Tango. She had no doubt in her mind now for she recognized the white sock, grey with mud, the small neat star and the snippet between her nostrils. She let go of Suzy and ran shouting, "It's Tango. I've found Tango! Look, William, look!" The mare raised her head and whinnied, recognizing her voice. Another minute and Amanda had her arms round the mare's neck, tears streaming down her face, calling, "Look everyone, it's Tango. My long-lost Tango." But no one could hear because of the dogs barking.

The door was open now and a strange person stood looking at William. She had a hooked nose and eyes sunken in her head and she was small, and as thin as her animals, in a knitted cardigan, a wool skirt and an apron made out of a sack. Her thin hair was drawn back in a minute bun at the back of her head, and her hands and face were grey with dirt. She wore bedroom slippers on her feet and the whole shack reeked of the smell of cats and oil heaters.

"What is it? What do you want?" she asked.

"We're looking for a little girl," yelled William. "She's been lost since yesterday. Have you seen her?" A dog was nipping at his heels now and he was glad he was wearing boots. "There are lots of people looking – the police, a helicopter. It's very serious," he shouted.

Marvin was catching Suzy whom Amanda had left unattended. Alison was looking at the horses, wondering what they lived on, wondering how long it would be before they started dying of starvation.

"You had better come in," said the old lady to William.

He sat down on her bed, which was covered by pony skins, and tried to explain, while the dogs grew tired of barking and the cats stopped spitting.

"She's a strange child," he said. "She may be deaf."

"I haven't seen a child. I live here alone, quite alone. I have for thirty-odd years now. I just ride me old bicycle to the village five miles away for groceries once a week. Not that I need much. I live mostly on potatoes," said the old lady. She gave a strange crackling laugh and kept wiping her hands on her apron. All the time the dogs and cats were watching her, as though she was a sort of goddess.

"I had best be off, then," William said, standing up.

But now Amanda had braved the dogs and stood in the doorway, white-faced, shaking with a mixture of shock and emotion.

"I've found Tango," she said. "She's out there in the field. She recognized me." Tears were still streaming down her face. A thousand memories came back to her – winning the Combined Training at Pony Club Camp on Tango, hunting, riding cross-country, waking up in the morning early to ride before school. She had been missing Tango for more than a year. But she had never stopped looking; nor had she given up hope of finding her eventually.

"Are you sure?" asked William, joining her by the door.

"Yes." Amanda was almost choking with emotion.

"One hundred per cent sure?"

"Yes. She's got bits of white in all the right places. And we know each other – we do really. It's like a miracle," cried Amanda.

"We'd better send for the police, then," said William.

"We can't. I can't leave her here a minute longer. She could die in the night. I've got to take her home," cried Amanda.

"We can't yet," William said.

"Your father can meet me half-way with the cattle truck. I'll start now. I've worked it all out,' argued Amanda.

"We came here to find a lost child."

"I don't care. She knew me. She neighed. She looked at me with such hope on her face, I can't leave her. I'd rather die," said Amanda, still crying. Marvin was calling from outside: "Are you coming? It's nearly eleven. We haven't much time left."

Amanda took hold of William's arm. "If you won't help, I'll go it alone," she said.

"You talk to the old lady, I'll go outside and talk to the others," he answered. It was ten forty-five now and the rain had started again. "Amanda won't leave because she thinks she's found her horse. Will you two go on to the sea? It's straight ahead. Then come straight back here. If we're not here, ride for the cattle truck. You know the way, don't you?" he said.

"Yes of course," replied Alison. "We've got maps anyway. Don't worry, William. I'm just so glad for Amanda."

"We won't stay long by the sea. It's getting late and look at the rain. It's all just a wash-out," Marvin said.

"Keep looking," William said. "She may be washed up on the beach."

They started trotting away. There was no one else to be seen, nothing but the sickly animals and birds swooping low, strange birds which William had never seen before.

"Where did you get the beautiful part-bred Arab mare?" Amanda was asking now inside the shack, sitting on the pony skins, with cats settling on her knees and dogs gnawing at her shoes.

"Well, that *is* a long story," cackled the old lady. "Would you like a cuppa before I begin?"

"No, thank you, we haven't much time," answered William from the doorway.

"I've rescued all of them, every one of the animals here," said the old lady proudly. "See that cat there . . .?"

"Can you tell us about the mare?" asked William, while Mulberry neighed by the gate. "Where was *she*, when you rescued her?"

"A young man brought her. Ever such a nice young man. It must have been a year ago last Michaelmas. He said she was going to the abattoir and would I save her. He said he worked there and she was too nice for meat, and he was packing the whole thing in. He said he would come back for her, but he never has. He was such a nice young man, too," said the old lady.

"She's mine," replied Amanda. "I can prove it."

"I wouldn't know anything about that. A young man brought her here, just like I said. I'm not a liar," replied the old woman.

"I'll handle this," said William. "She was stolen from Amanda here, Granny, do you understand? Taken away one night."

"I wouldn't know anything about that. It was like I said," replied the old lady, wiping her hands on her apron. "I'm not a granny either."

"We're getting nowhere," said Amanda, with despair in her voice.

"I wouldn't like you to take her. Supposing the young man came back for her, how would I look then?"

"I'll give you my address. I'll write you a note to give him. I'll pay him for her if he comes back, I promise," cried Amanda.

"Can you let us have a bit of paper?" asked William.

"I'll look." She started to fumble in drawers. All the time minutes were passing, and the rain was beating harder and harder on the window panes.

"I haven't got a halter," Amanda said.

"We'll fix up something," replied William.

"Our saddles will be soaked. Or rather *your* saddles. I'm so sorry," Amanda said.

"Don't worry."

"Now for a pencil," said the old woman.

"I suppose Tango would have ended up just another skin on this bed," whispered Amanda.

The paper had lines on it and the pencil had no point, but at last Amanda was writing her address and telephone number, adding: "IOU one part-bred chestnut mare."

"She had a halter, he brought a halter with her. Just let me look," said the old woman, taking the piece of paper. She searched under the bed, while cats crawled near her, purring. Then she looked in the porch and came back with a tattered hemp halter. "Here you are, dear," she said. "That's Minnie's. That's what I call her, Minnie. All their names begin with M. There's Marigold and Maisie and Mrs Mop and old Marmaduke and Maple Leaf and . . ."

"Thank you so much," said William.

"Can you manage?"

"Yes. Don't come out. You'll only get wet," said William.

"Oh, I don't mind a bit of rain. It will wash me hair," she replied, cackling.

"I can't wait to get Tango home," said Amanda over her shoulder, running towards the field. "I shall have the vet over straight away. She'll have everything money will buy – linseed, boiled barley, clover hay, louse powder, the lot."

"Not all at once. Or you'll kill her. She'll get colic. You'll have to build her up slowly," William answered, following.

Mulberry and Suzy were still tied to the gate. The wind had dropped.

"Tango. Darling Tango," said Amanda, slipping the halter over her ears. "We're going home."

"It's almost eleven and there's nearly ten kilometres to go. Hurry," shouted William, but he knew they couldn't hurry with Tango. She was too

emanciated, she might never make the journey at all.

"She hasn't any shoes," said Amanda.

"It doesn't matter, the ground's soft. Do you want me to lead her? Mulberry's quieter than Suzy."

Amanda handed him the halter rope. One of the horses in the field was lying down. He looked as though he would never get up again.

"We'll have to send the R.S.P.C.A. here. There's nothing else we can do," William said.

He wondered where the others were. Had they reached the sea yet? Perhaps he should have ridden on alone. Amanda was mounting Suzy now, saying, "God, she looks awful! Do you think she'll survive the journey?"

"I don't know, I just don't know," William said.

They blew their whistles, short and quick, but the rain seemed to deaden sound and there was no answering blast.

"We must hurry," William said, pulling at Tango. A horse in one of the fields whinnied and the dogs started to bark again.

"I can't even hear the sea any more," said Amanda.

"The wind's dropped and the clouds are coming down," replied William, and they both knew what that meant – fog!

Chapter Four

A job worth doing

"I suppose we have to go on," Marvin said.

"William said so," replied Alison.

"He's not God."

"I know, but he is in charge."

"Then why isn't he here?"

"Because Amanda's found her long-lost horse. That's important too. Put yourself in her place. Supposing it was Skinflint there, instead of Tango? How would you feel?" asked Alison.

"I would want him put down at once. Every animal there should be put down. There's no hope for any of them. Can't you understand?" said Marvin.

He hated sick animals and he could feel his asthma beginning. Ten minutes more and he would be choking for air.

"I can't go on. I'm getting asthma. I shall have to turn back," he said.

"I'm going on. I'm going on alone, then," answered Alison, who never accepted defeat. "I am not going back."

"The sea always gives me asthma. It's the sudden change of air. Hang on. I've got a tablet somewhere." He searched his pockets and found the envelope with the medicine in it but the tablets were now just a soggy mess.

"They've got wet," he said with despair in his voice.

"Go back then. I don't care. I like being alone," shouted Alison. She was trotting now and she could hear the waves beating against rocks. And the rain was lashing her face, daring her to go on.

"I can't leave you," Marvin said.

"I'll be all right. I don't want you to die of asthma," shouted Alison, with scorn in her voice. She thought of her mother just back from working in the hospital. She would be tired. She would go straight to bed with a sleeping pill. Her brothers would be out working. No one would notice when she returned so it didn't matter. The lost child mattered much more. She had to be found. Alison's mother was always saying "If a job's worth doing, it's worth doing properly." Alison had been brought up to take orders and carry them out and she was not changing now.

Behind her Marvin was blowing his nose, praying, "God make my asthma go away," and shouting, "Wait, hang on a minute."

But Alison simply cantered on towards the sea. Suddenly the soil changed and the thick dark earth was gone; there was wiry grass sprouting from sandy earth, and no more cabbages or rotting potatoes and over everything hung the wonderful smell of the sea. Alison started to sing the Skye Boat Song; now the rain didn't matter any more. She was alone and happy, thinking about Amanda and William – how kind and nice Amanda is, she thought, and William is really good-looking. She imagined dancing with him, riding home from a long day's hunting, asking him over to listen to her cassettes. Her mother would like him. He wasn't stuck up like Marvin. He was what her mother called 'genuine'. He would find her home rather small and shabby, but he wouldn't mind because he wasn't that sort of person. He liked the great outdoors. As for Amanda, she was destined to be Alison's best friend. They would go shopping together, buy books, records, tapes, clothes. They would meet and ride together. The sound of the sea was growing louder now. Rainbow sniffed the air and stopped.

"It's only the sea, silly, the beautiful sea," cried Alison.

Tango trotted as best she could, but she soon grew tired. Lack of food made her weak and her hoofs were split and sore and every time Amanda looked at the poverty marks in her quarters, she felt like crying.

William looked at his watch. "It's after twelve o'clock already. We'll never make the cattle truck by one. There's at least eight kilometres to go, and just look at Tango," he said. He felt like screaming. He felt trapped, a failure. There was no sign of Marvin and Alison. Supposing they never turned up? The skies seemed to be descending, clouds whirled above their heads and there was a rawness in the air which ate deep into their bones. He thought of his father, probably waiting already. He would get out of the cab and walk up and down, swinging his arms to keep warm. He hated waiting. He would be wanting to be home by milking time.

William jerked at Tango's rope and shouted,

"Come on," and she tried to trot and almost fell.

"She can't go any faster," shrieked Amanda, wondering now whether Tango would ever reach home. And, if they reached the cattle truck, how would she stand the last lap? She might fall down in the truck and never get up again. We're too late, she thought. I ought to have known of this place and come before. I should have asked more people, searched further. I always had the feeling she was still alive somewhere. The clouds seemed to be coming to meet them now, and somewhere in the distance a cow was lowing. William had to hold Mulberry back because Tango couldn't keep up with his walk any more. There was a look of anguish in her eyes and she was breathing harder than usual, so that short bursts of steam seemed to be coming from her nostrils. Then she started to sweat and her whole body sent volumes of steam into the raw air.

"I'd like to kill that old woman," cried Amanda suddenly. "I would like to chop her up in little bits."

"It wouldn't do any good. You'd be sent to a mental hospital and kept on sedatives and analysed. No one would understand, except possibly me," replied William.

"Would you stand up for me in court?"

"Of course. But the R.S.P.C.A. will deal with her. They'll put most of the amimals down, and then local authorities and local do-gooders will put her in an old people's home and she won't cackle any more," William said. "But do cheer up, we must have covered a couple of miles already, and if we don't take it too fast, I expect she'll make it. She's got the courage and the breeding."

"I'm sorry I'm such a fool. I should have left her until tomorrow, but I couldn't bear to lose her again," replied Amanda.

"Look, there's the farm, we're making quite good progress," said William, trying to sound cheerful.

"How long will it take to get her fat?" asked Amanda after a time.

"Two years at least. But she should get better as soon as you start feeding her. I'll help. We've got everything on the farm. I'll put some linseed on to boil and make her a bran mash with black treacle in it, and you can put glucose in her water too. I'll boil some barley for her as well, but we mustn't rush it. It'll take time," said William.

There were lights on in the farmhouse when they passed it again, though it was only one o'clock in the afternoon. They could hear a plane overhead now, flying high above the clouds.

"Our loosebox is full of junk because last winter Dad decided to make it into a workshop," Amanda said.

"That's all right, she can stay with us tonight. You can stay as well, if you like," William said.

They couldn't see much now, but the horses seemed to know where they were going, and at intervals William thought he recognized trees and bits of hedgerow. They came to the cabbage field and he shouted, "It's all right. We are still going the right way," and Amanda said, "I do hope they've found the little girl. If she spends another night out, she's sure to die."

Marvin was riding back alone. There was a rasping sound each time he breathed and he felt both sick and dizzy. Soon he felt faint too, and after that he simply gave Skinflint his head and prayed for help.

Skinflint tossed his head and set off at a mad gallop and in less than five minutes he had stopped at the old woman's place. Marvin felt like dying but he kicked Skinflint on, shouting in a desperate voice, "Go home. Go to the cattle truck, you fool. There's no one here." But it wasn't really his own voice which came out because of his asthma. He could feel the fog coming now, swirling round his head, trying to suffocate him. But, in the end, desperation gave him strength and after a few moments Skinflint was galloping again, while Marvin held onto the saddle with both hands, praying for deliverance. Presently he passed into a dream-like state and he imagined himself at home with his mother rushing him to bed, fetching hot water bottles, phoning for Doctor Beatty.

Alison was there, too, saying, "I didn't believe him. I didn't know. I didn't understand." William was kneeling by the bed praying, while Alison stood by the window saying, "It's all my fault."

Then the scene changed and he was lying downstairs on the sofa with uncles and aunts and his granny all looking at him and he thought, this is the end. They've come because it's the end.

Skinflint was trotting now, his ears pricked listening, his eyes trying to pierce the descending fog. It felt strange to Marvin. He opened his eyes and saw the fog and suddenly he knew where he was. He put his hand in his pocket and put his whistle to his lips and blew and blew, but there was no answer of any kind, just damp, marshy fields, with no one to be seen anywhere.

* * *

Alison had reached a precipice. She stood up in her stirrups and looked down and saw the sea crashing against rocks in a kind of fury as though it wanted to kill them. She still felt happy.

"Well, that's that then," she told Rainbow. "Mission completed." She patted his neck and thinking of Tango said, "Thank God it wasn't you."

Her watch said twelve o'clock and she knew now that she couldn't possibly be back by one. She thought, when I get home I shall have a long hot bath and a mug of hot chocolate. She started to sing again as she turned for home, and it was then she thought she heard a voice calling, "Here, here, here."

She halted Rainbow and listened, but all she could hear now were the crashing waves. I'm going mad imagining things, she thought, and I haven't time. I must ride fast and furiously, gallop faster than I've ever before or I shall be lost in the fog which is coming. I *must* find the cattle truck. Then the cry came again. "Here, here, Maggy here," and suddenly she was on her feet running towards the cliff top, peering down to where she could see something bright which turned out to be a piece of red scarf against some dark hair.

"I'm coming," she said. "Don't worry. I'll just tie up my horse."

But there was nothing to tie him too. Suddenly Alison was consumed by a sense of panic. If only William was with her, Marvin, anyone, she thought. She unbuckled the reins and undid the studbillets on one side, then buckled them together again. There was a boulder just over the cliff. She decided to tie Rainbow to it. She started talking to him, "Rainbow, this is the greatest moment of your life. You must be good. You mustn't move. You must stay. I can't get back without you." He pricked his ears and smelt her hands. "You understand, don't you? Be good, please," she said.

She had to lean over the cliff to put the end of the reins under the boulder. Below, the sea rose and fell with tremendous fury.

"Stand now. Stand," she said.

She leaned over and looked at the child. She needed a rope – help – but there wasn't any. She tried blowing her whistle again and again until her lips split in the wind. Then she took off the belt of her riding waterproof and gave it to Maggy to hold. She gave her the buckle end and she wasn't far over the side, just two or three feet. A normal child could make it with ease. But would Maggy understand what she had to do? Alison had no idea. "In a minute I'm going to pull, you scramble up. Okay?" she said. The child was wearing nothing but a dress and cardigan, she had lost her socks and shoes somewhere on the way. She looked like a small animal curled up above the sea.

"Ready. Heave ho!" shouted Alison, and Maggy crawled up like a rabbit in little jumps. Alison took off her waterproof and coat and put the coat on Maggy because the waterproof was far too big. Rainbow was watching them. Maggy was shaking with cold, her teeth chattering, her face, hands and feet were blue. "We are going home, back to Granny," said Alison.

She knew she mustn't put a foot wrong. One mistake and Maggy would run, one quick move and Rainbow would leap back and be gone. "You're going to ride," she said. "Here, have my hat. Put it on." She undid Rainbow, talking to him in the same voice, saying, "Everything's going to be all right."

Maggy was playing with the hat. Alison leant down and put it on her head. Then she lifted her straight on to Rainbow's back, and now she could have cried with relief. "Home," she said. "Hold on to the saddle, Maggy."

But Maggy's hands were too cold to hold on to anything, so Alison pushed them up her coat sleeves and said, "Walk," to Rainbow, and slowly they set off. Maggy was saying, "Ride," and humming a little tune to herself and Alison thought, "It's all right. Everything is going to be all right."

Chapter Five

"Where are the others?"

Tango was simply putting one hoof in front of the other now, while William was trying to sing, but the fog was in his throat and his voice came out muffled.

"Shall I go on and fetch the cattle truck?" asked Amanda. They had crossed the cabbage fields; there was an old shed on their left and a quarry on their right. The fog was growing thicker each passing second. They had stopped talking, because there seemed nothing left to say.

William shook his head. "The wheels can't grip on this sort of ground. They would simply spin round," he said.

It was one fifteen now. William wondered how many people were waiting for them. Had Mr Metcalf gone home leaving his father in charge? Had the other riders turned up safely? Had the little girl been found?

Amanda was walking now, saying, "Suzy's tired. You take her. I'll walk with Tango."

She walked with one arm round Tango's neck talking to her, willing her to survive the last few miles. She imagined her mother standing at the window in the sitting room, looking out. Presently she would telephone the farm to say, "Aren't they home yet? Have you seen the fog outside, Mrs Gaze? It's a real pea-souper."

She always said people's names. She liked to be addressed in the same way – by name. Would she be pleased to see Tango? Amanda wondered next. And what about her father? He wouldn't like the bills for food, and shoes and worm powders. He would say his bank account was empty and hadn't Amanda ever heard of income tax?

Far away now they could see dim lights shining at them as though through cotton wool. I shall have to get a job, decided Amanda. I'll be a waitress, or a domestic help or something. Dad will never pay all the bills. Tango was stumbling again now, and presently she fell right over and lay in the mud panting. "Leave her for a bit. Let her rest," William said, dismounting, with despair in his voice.

"She's going to die. She's dying isn't she?" yelled Amanda.

"No, let her rest."

Amanda went down on her knees beside Tango, cradling her lovely chestnut head in her lap, saying, "You're going to be all right. We're nearly there. Just half a mile more."

William loosened Mulberry's girths and felt pangs of hunger gnawing at his own stomach.

"If no one had found the girl, she'll be dead by the morning," he said.

But Amanda had thoughts only for Tango now. "Why don't you fetch the cattle truck? Can't you see she can't go any further?" she yelled.

"It's on the last bit of hard-core road. It hasn't

four-wheel drive like a Landrover," he said.

"You could try at least," she said.

"It hasn't field tyres either. Why don't you believe me?" he asked.

"I don't want to. I don't want to leave Tango here to die."

"She'll get up in a minute, when she's ready."

"She's dying. And you don't care."

He knelt down beside Tango in the mud. She was still breathing, but not in the right way. Her sides seemed to be fluttering in and out, and she was very still – too still. Suddenly William didn't know what to do. He could go on for help. Find a tractor to pull the cattle truck, but he might never find Amanda again, for the fog was growing thicker each moment and William knew it was going to stay all night, right round until the start of another day.

He tried blowing his whistle, but there were no answering sounds.

"I'll go on a bit. Don't move," he said. "I'll take Suzy with me and try to find help." He looked around for a landmark, but there was nothing, not a tree, or a hedge, not even a piece of rusty wire. Just mud.

Amanda was sitting down close to Tango. "Hurry," she said. "Please hurry."

Marvin could see the cattle truck now. He wanted to cheer, but he had no breath to cheer with. The back was down. There was no sign of anyone. He dismounted slowly, his breath still coming in gasps. He put Skinflint's rug on and a head collar and led him up the ramp. His legs felt weak and he was overcome with dizziness, which made him sit down for a time. But at last Skinflint was tied up. He staggered down the ramp and clambered into the cab and started to pour himself coffee with shaking hands. He thought, I've made it, and for the moment that was all that mattered.

"Well done, Maggy," said Alison. "You're doing very well. You'll soon be home with your granny, eating a lovely tea – iced cakes, malt bread and butter, biscuits." She was walking in a kind of daze now, and the ground was wet and salty and water splashed her boots. Although she didn't know yet, the sea was coming in, flooding the land . . . She wished Maggy would talk. It was eerie and unnerving never to get an answer. It was like talking to a blank wall. But she went on talking just the same.

"Isn't Rainbow great?" she said. "He's won lots of rosettes, more than fifty. He jumps beautifully and he's won working hunter classes. Would you like to jump, Maggy? It's great fun, it is really. Perhaps one day you'll let me teach you. How about that?"

She didn't expect an answer any more. She started to think about home, about her mother leaving a shopping list for her on the table and expecting supper when she woke up.

Then she turned round and saw that Maggy wasn't on Rainbow any more. She stared at an empty saddle, and shouted, "Oh God, what now? Isn't everything bad enough?" before she started to call, "Maggy, Maggy! Where are you?" though she knew that there would be no answer, and her voice echoed and the echo seemed to mock her. She turned Rainbow round and started to walk back the way she had come, and Rainbow stopped and jibbed and wouldn't walk. Alison stopped then and started to shout. "William, Amanda, where are you? William, Marvin. I need you. William," until all the words ran into each other. But only the sea gull answered with a distant cry.

Then Alison looked down and saw for the first time, that the sea was washing her boots. She was filled with panic. She started to hit Rainbow then, to scream, "Come on, damn you. She'll drown, you fool." the day seemed to have lasted for years already. She ran back, dragging Rainbow, and soon she could hear the roar of the sea again. Why does everything have to go wrong for me, she thought with anguish. I must be cursed. She could see now how tired Rainbow was and she wondered whether the others had reached the cattle truck yet and how long they would wait for her. And now she could feel salt on her cheeks and she knew she was crying, not as she usually did, with rage and frustration, but with a kind of hopelessness. I should have looked, she thought. I should have held on to her. I can't go back home now and say I found her and then lost her. She'll drown, and it will be my fault. I can't live with that. I can't endure it. She tried yelling, "Marvin!" but no one answered. The fog obliterated everything. It was like walking with your head wrapped in a blanket. There was no escaping, no way out. And no giving up, Alison decided. I must go on searching until I drop, because I would rather die than go back now without Maggy.

Amanda's mother was ringing up Mrs Gaze.

"Any news?" she asked. "I've just turned on the

radio and thre was nothing at all, Mrs Gaze. When do you think they will be back?"

"Any minute," replied Mrs Gaze. "My husband left at eleven. He should be back any minute. Not to worry. William's got a lot of sense, Amanda will be all right with him."

"I'll keep her dinner warm in the oven then, Mrs Gaze," said Amanda's mother. "There's a terrible fog here. It was forecast, wasn't it?"

"That's right. Not to worry," replied Mrs Gaze. "They will drop Amanda on the way. My husband is used to fog. He'll drive slowly."

Mrs Carruthers was back from the hospital. There was no sign of Alison. She put on the radio and there was no mention of the lost child either. She made herself some coffee and waited. She could see fog coming down outside. There had been a pile-up on the motorway during the morning involving forty cars, with two drivers killed. She didn't know whom to telephone about Alison. She opened the door and looked out and now she could hardly see the road outside. The police should have sent them home. They should have been warned, she thought. I shall sue whoever is responsible if Alison's hurt.

"So here you are," said Mr Gaze, looking up at Marvin in the cab. "Where are the others?"

"On their way," replied Marvin, breathing as though he had just ran a mile without stopping. "We had to separate. I had to come back because of my asthma. I kept feeling sick."

"You look it too," replied Mr Gaze. "You look in a proper mess, son. It's long past one o'clock. The police have gone, there's only Mr Metcalf and me left. Everyone else is on their way home. What's happened to you? Where are William and the girls?"

Marvin wanted to explain, but the more he thought about the horrors of the last few hours, the worse his asthma became.

"I didn't want to come home," he panted, "I wanted to stay with Alison, like William said. But I couldn't breathe any more. I've vomitted three times. What Mum will say I can't imagine, and Skinflint's all run up and covered with mud and I can't brush him like I am. And Amanda would insist a terrible horse was her long-lost one, and now here I am and I feel awful. I wish I could die."

"Take it easy. They'll be all right," replied Mr Gaze as calmly as he could. "I just wish I hadn't told the police everything was under control. William's never let me down before. I never expected it."

"It's all Amanda's fault. She's crazy," gasped Marvin.

Mr Gaze walked up and down. He had taken tablets to dull the pain from his arthritis and they made him sleepy. It was two o'clock now, and William had never been late like this before. "The news mentioned flooding. I hope they're not still down by the sea," he said.

Marvin had his eyes shut now. He was only half conscious. His breathing seemed to be coming from his stomach, and his face was the colour of putty. Presently Mr Metcalf appeared out of the fog with a torch.

"Not back yet?" he said, making a tut-tutting noise. "Looks as thought we'll be here all night. Do you mind if I go back home for an hour or so, my wife will by worrying? She expected me for lunch."

"That's all right. There's nothing one can do but wait. This fog isn't going to clear by nightfall," replied Mr Gaze.

Marvin was asleep now, dreaming that he was being pursued by a small girl screaming, "You didn't wait. I'm telling the police you didn't wait."

She had huge yellow teeth and her bones stuck up out of her flesh. He woke up to find beads of sweat on his face, unable to think where he was.

"I thought I heard hoofs just now," said Mr Gaze. "They can't be much longer."

"What's the time?" asked Marvin.

"Half past two."

It felt much later. Outside, one could see nothing but fog.

"I ought to telephone Mum," said Marvin.

"The nearest telephone box is over a mile away," replied Mr Gaze, "and I don't think you are in any condition to walk that far."

Chapter Six

A journey through mud

Tango was standing up now, trembling and whinnying, afraid to be left alone with Amanda in the fog and the dark. Amanda shouted, "Wait, William. Come back. She's better."

The sea smell was stronger now, nearer; the air seemed full of salt.

"Wait, William, wait," screamed Amanda again.

His voice came back at last, muffled by fog. "I'm waiting," he called.

"Walk, come on, walk," said Amanda. It was very muddy and the mud clung to her boots making them feel heavier each moment. Tango was walking again now and her breathing seemed easier.

"Any sign of the others?" called Amanda.

"Not so far," William was standing waiting, swearing under his breath, wishing the day was over. "Hurry, do hurry," he shouted. There was no other sound at all, as though they were the only people left in the whole world.

"It's the mud, it's dragging us both down," called Amanda. She had nearly reached him now. She looked pale and tired, and she carried great clods of earth on her boots.

"If the child hasn't been found by now, she will be dead," said William. "What a day!"

"We will never forget it," said Amanda.

"You're telling me."

"At least we've got Tango. I still can't believe it. Do you remember how she used to look? I won a rosette for Best Turn Out and Condition on her, do you remember?"

"Best Rider, too," added William.

"What a day that was! And you won the Handy Hunter on Boxer, and the cup for the most points in the gymkhana events on Suzy."

"Those were the days," agreed William, and he mourned them now for suddenly he felt years older.

"I hope the others are there when we reach the cattle truck," he said.

"They must be. Alison's no fool. She's great. We must have her in the Patrol. We need new blood," Amanda answered.

He thought about the Patrol as he put one foot in front of the other, and Suzy and Mulberry walked beside him matching their strides to his. How long would it last? he wondered. He had thought their fight against fire had been hard, but this was worse. This was a fight against life and death, he thought, because if we don't reach the cattle truck soon, we'll be lost, walking in circles, and no one will ever find us. We'll just be a few more people lost in the marshes for ever.

"Do you remember the day hounds ran ten miles?" Amanda asked. "How we galloped side by side and at the end there was just us and the huntsman and Tango and Boxer? We never checked once. That was a wonderful day, wasn't it?"

"Yes, I remember," said William, "and there was a ten kilometre hack back to the boxes."

"That's right. Do you remember, Tango? Do you?" Amanda was kissing the mare's neck now, urging her on. She looked like a scarecrow, like a clothes horse dressed as a horse, thought William, like a ghost coming out of the fog – a ghost from better days, perhaps we will all be ghosts soon, thought William. Perhaps we will roam the marshes on dark nights wailing, Amanda and me and our three exhausted horses.

"What's the time?" called Amanda after a few minutes.

William had to wait for her. Tango was hardly walking now, just staggering along like a drunkard.

"Half past two," he said.

"Mum will be having kittens. Help!" cried Amanda.

"My grandfather was in the trenches in the Great War," said William. "He used to say that in the end, what with the mud and the filth and the horses dying in the lines, you didn't mind if you died yourself – half of you wanted to die, just to escape. I feel a bit like that myself. I don't care any more," said William.

"But we're not going to die. We're nearly there. In a minute we'll see the lights of the cattle truck," cried Amanda.

"In a minute, your mare is going to die," said William. "Look at her. She's barely moving."

Alison knew she was walking in circles but somewhere in a circle there might be Maggy. She had stopped calling because she had no breath left. All the time the sea seemed to be coming in, covering the wiry grass, coming and going as relentlessy as time passing. Each minute it seemed to be coming in a little further, covering more ground, and the air was full of water, dripping through the fog.

And then at last she saw Maggy in a huddled heap, her hands over her head. She was afraid to touch her, afraid of what she might see, so she asked, "Are you all right, Maggy? Are you? Say something please."

She didn't really expect an answer. Rainbow kept backing away, pulling towards home. She shouted, "Stand" at him, and knelt down. Turning Maggy over, she said, "Are you all right?" Maggy had her eyes firmly shut and now she pushed her fists into them. But there were no pools of blood, no broken limbs.

"We are going on. We are going home," Alison said.

She felt enclosed and completely alone in the fog. She picked up Maggy and put her on Rainbow's back. There was no sign of her riding hat. "We are going home," she said again, walking backwards watching Maggy. "So don't get off, because I'm not going back for you again."

Rainbow knew which way to go. For a while they seemed to be splashing through the sea and then there was just a sea of mud which dragged at them both. Maggy was shivering. She looked small and shrivelled and sometimes hardly alive.

"We'll soon be home," said Alison, without much conviction. She thought, if we hurry the truck will still be waiting, Mr Gaze won't go without us. Probably the police will be there too. We're going to be all right. She looked at her watch and it was half past two. If we hurry we'll be back by four, she thought. And they *must* wait. They *can't* go without us. Her boots felt impossibly heavy and now she was starting to feel weak. Eight more miles, she thought. I can always ride with Maggy on my knees, if I can't walk any more.

Mum will be asleep by now, she thought, and my lunch will still be waiting in the oven. She tried to walk faster but it wasn't possible in the mud, she had to go step by step, she had to reserve her strength or she would never make it.

If only I had some chocolate, something to give us both some energy, she thought. Suddenly she could see the shack with the horses standing like ghosts behind their wire fences with nothing to do and nothing to eat.

She turned to Maggy then and said, "House. Food. Look." And she started to shout, "Anyone at home?" The dogs barked, and she saw that water was rising everywhere, washing the doorstep. She tied Rainbow to the gate and carried Maggy in her arms to the front door calling "Help. We need help." The dogs barked louder still. She banged on the door and there was water washing her boots. "Open up," she yelled. "You're going to be flooded. Open the door."

Then Maggy started to scream. It was a scream of sheer terror, and there seemed to be dogs everywhere sniffing at their heels and snarling. Alison started back down the path, muttering, "It's all right. I've got you. You are going to be all right." She thought, they'll all be drowned, the old woman, dogs, cats, horses even, but what can I do? a terrier bit her heel through her boot as she walked, and she could feel blood running into her

sock. It didn't hurt because her feet had been numb for the last two hours.

"I can see the truck!" yelled William. "Look there – just ahead. We've made it. We're going to be all right." Now he was running and his father was calling, "About time too. Have you got Amanda? Fine, we'll be off then. We're all set. Marvin's in the cab. Whatever happened?"

"We've got Tango too. We've found her," yelled William.

"What? Amanda's old pony?"

"Yes."

William was pulling off the tack now, with numb hands, putting on head collars and Amanda was coming through the fog, coaxing a dying Tango, promising her oats, bran mashes, deep beds of golden straw.

"She's all in," said Mr Gaze. "Here, let me give you a hand, Mandy."

"She's nearly dead," gasped Amanda. "I'll stay with her. If she dies I want to be with her."

They half carried Tango into the cattle truck.

"Marvin's half dead too," said Mr Gaze. "He needs a doctor."

"What about the little girl?" asked William.

"They haven't found her. They've given up hope."

They loaded Suzy and Mulberry and threw up the ramp.

"Marvin looks awful. His breathing's terrible," said Mr Gaze.

William could hardly stand now. Everything seemed to be going round and round. Mr Metcalf called, "Are you all right, then?" He carried a lantern.

And Mr Gaze shouted back, "Yes, sir. All aboard?"

"Thank God we're all here," said William.

Marvin still had his eyes shut.

A police car drifted through the fog and a policeman tapped on the cab window asking "All right? Everyone accounted for?" and Mr Gaze yelled, "Yes, but we've got a sick boy and a dying horse," and starting the engine, drove through the mud with wheels spinning.

"I thought you weren't going to make it," he said. "I thought you were all done for."

"We nearly didn't," replied William.

"I want to be sick," said Marvin.

"We're nearly home, just another hour," answered Mr Gaze.

They could see the road now. Lights, sanity.

"Pity they didn't find the girl," said Mr Gaze.

"Did you get on all right with Alison, Marvin?" William asked.

"Yes, until my asthma came," wheezed Marvin.

William poured himself coffee, ate sandwiches and fruit cake and the horrors of being lost in the fog started to fade. He thought of home, of sitting by the fire and drying out, of sleep.

"We ought to give the others something to eat in the truck," he said.

"They'll be all right," replied Mr Gaze. "We're late enough without stopping."

Tango was still standing up, leaning heavily against the partitions of the cattle truck, hardly breathing at times. Amanda stood near to her, watching every breath, thinking of nothing else, praying, "God, make her live, please God." She was very tired. Several times she nearly fell asleep standing up watching her horse, remembering the life they had shared together. She looked at her poor split hoofs, and and her thin neck and threadbare mane, at her rump which rose from her quarters in a peak instead of being fat and round, and she thought, we were only just in time. Another few days and she might have been dead. She handed Tango wisps of hay from the hay-net and wondered whether the hollows above her eyes would ever disappear.

It was nearly dark now, and she couldn't see the other horses. She imagined that Alison had arrived before them, that Rainbow was somewhere in the truck and that Alison was in the cab with the others. After a time, her legs gave way, and sinking into the straw, she slept, dreaming of the house with the old lady and the pony skins.

And in the front, William and Marvin slept too and slowly, insidiously, dusk came creeping across the flat fields.

"Poor kids, they're all done in," thought Mr Gaze, driving on through village after village, headlights blazing, taking the corners slowly because he had a full load. All the time the fog seemed to be growing thicker, and the day darker. William was muttering now in his sleep saying, "Tell the R.S.P.C.A. And, yes, cats. I said *cats*."

Marvin was still breathing in gasps, but there was no noise from the truck. The girls must be asleep, thought Mr Gaze. Just as well. They're all dead tired.

Chapter Seven

I feel so ill

"We're past the farm now, Maggy, we're nearly there," Alison said. She was riding now with Maggy sitting on her knee. Rainbow was walking on a loose rein finding his own way through the fog by instinct, never hesitating. Alison imagined their arrival. Everyone will cheer when the see Maggy, she thought. We'll be given hot drinks and Maggy's granny will be there waiting. It seemed years since the morning and now Alison's watch had stopped, but it didn't matter any more, nothing mattered compared with the fact that she had Maggy safe and warm in her arms. Mission completed successfully, she thought. She started to sing, childish songs she had learned when she was small, like *This Old Man* and *Little Bo Peep* and *Now the Day is Over*. Then she started to sing carols, and Maggy hummed in a tuneless way and Alison was happy, happier than she had been for ages.

I can't wait for a hot bath, she thought. Rainbow will have to survive deep litter tonight, just more bed on top of the old. No one can be angry with me when they see Maggy, no one can complain, and now she was singing *God Save the Queen* and *There's no Place like Home* at the top of her voice, and Rainbow pricked his ears and jogged and she could see faraway lights and hear faraway trains. Even Mum can't be cross when she knows I found Maggy, she thought. She can never say I'm faint-hearted again.

The ground was growing harder under Rainbow's hoofs. The sea was long behind them. Alison started to call, "Coo-ee. Anyone there? It's me – Alison. I've got Maggy." And Rainbow's hoofs made a hard sound on the ground now.

Suddenly, there was the bunker, telegraph wires at the end of a road. "This is it!" thought Alison. "But where are they?" She halted Rainbow. "Anyone at home?" she yelled, with mounting panic. "Anyone there?" She could feel her heart pounding against her ribs now. Maggy sensed her distress and started to scream and struggle.

"Stop it!" shouted Alison. "Stop, please, stop it!"

Maggy was fighting now with fiendish strength, trying to throw herself off, screaming, "I want Granny," Then Rainbow lost his nerve and started to buck and suddenly Alison was on the ground with Maggy underneath her, and there seemed nothing but stars rushing to meet her and a great thundering in her ears. She thought, I mustn't pass out. I must stay here because of Maggy. I can't faint now. But she could hear Rainbow's hoofs disappearing along the tarmac. The fog was everywhere and she held on to Maggy as the thundering and the stars stopped and everything went black.

"We'll stop at Alison's first, then, shall we, or Marvin's?" asked Mr Gaze.

"Drop me first, please," said Marvin. "I feel so ill. Please, Mr Gaze." He had always had a sharp nose, now it looked ever sharper and his eyes looked swollen.

"Right you are, so you shall be," replied Mr Gaze, "seeing that Alison isn't here in the cab to object."

Marvin's mother was waiting for him in the road.

"At last!" she cried in her loud voice. "What happened? You're hours late?"

"I'll unbox Skinflint," William said, climbing out of the cab.

"Marvin was taken ill, he needs to keep warm," said Mr Gaze. "My boy will put his pony away. Don't you worry, madam."

Amanda was still asleep. Tango was still standing up. "I'll unload Skinflint the front way," William said. "Otherwise I'll have to move the others." It was a struggle getting him out. He looked stiff and tired and his legs and hoofs were clogged with mud.

Meanwhile, Marvin's mother was taking Marvin indoors muttering under her breath, saying, "Where's your inhaler, Marvin? Why didn't you take it with you? You are a fool." He was gasping like a fish out of water.

William found a rug and put it on Skinflint. He filled up a water bucket and fetched hay.

"They'll have to give him his hard feed," he said, climbing back into the cab. "I can't do it all. Next stop home. Amanda wants to stay with us. Her Dad's turned the loosebox into a workshop. You know how he is . . . " Home, he thought, home at last!

"She didn't ask about the little girl," complained Mr Gaze.

"I expect she was worried about Marvin," replied William. Home, he thought. Oh to be home and out of the fog and the wet and the terrible mud. Pity we failed, he thought next, but we can't always win. Life isn't like that. You can't win all your battles. The lights were on again at the farm when they arrived and the cows were being milked. William felt as though he had been away on a long journey and come home, though it was only thirteen hours since they had been loading up, filled with hope.

He unboxed Mulberry; then Suzy. Amanda woke up and stared at Tango. "I thought I had dreamt it, but she's here, still alive,"she gasped.

"That's right. Let's get her out and prepare a bran mash. Gently does it," William said.

Tango staggered down the ramp, blinked under the yard light.

"I've been asleep, haven't I?" Amanda asked.

"That's right," said William.

"I feel as though I've been away years."

"Same here," said William.

"Is Marvin all right?"

"I think so."

They put Tango in a box, fetched her hay and water, put a rug on her, took a bucket of bran indoors. "Gosh I'm tired," exclaimed William. "We've got to do something about the other horses we left behind," Amanda said.

"I'll ring the R.S.P.C.A." William answered. "But it will have to wait until the morning. We need some glucose for Tango's water, and we must start boiling linseed for tomorrow."

"Tomorrow's Sunday," remembered Amanda. "The R.S.P.C.A. may not operate on Sundays."

"All right, I'll telephone soon."

"Then there's the dogs and cats," continued Amanda.

"Let's settle Tango and the others first," pleaded William, rubbing his eyes. "I feel as though I'll collapse any minute."

They were all in a state of collapse. Mrs Gaze gave them cups of strong tea well laced with sugar. William wouldn't sit down.

"If I sit down I shall never get up again," he said.

Mr Gaze disappeared to help with the milking. It was dark now but the fog was going at last.

"I must telephone my mother," Amanda said. "She'll come and fetch me."

They took Tango a bran mash and watched her eat it. William had grated apple into it and laced it with sliced carrot and a pound of black treacle.

"We'll get the vet in the morning to give her an injection of Vitamin B. I think she'll last the night," he said.

Mulberry was eating steadily with the munch of a healthy horse. Suzy was looking about her listening, knowing there was a stranger in one of the stables. The cows were going back to the fields now.

"I don't know how to thank you," began Amanda.

"Don't then," said William quickly. "I like having Tango."

"I'll come and muck her out first thing," promised Amanda. "Don't touch her in the morning."

"Telephone! It's Mrs Carruthers," called William's mother. "She's asking for Alison."

"For Alison?" cried William. "Didn't we drop her off? Where is she?"

"She's not at home," called Mrs Gaze. "Will you come and speak?"

"She was in the back with you, wasn't she?" asked William, staring at Amanda.

"Was she? I didn't see her. I was asleep a lot of the time."

"Didn't she box up with Marvin?" asked William, walking slowly towards the house, his legs suddenly weak at the knees.

"I thought she was in the cab with you," said Amanda.

"And I thought she was in the back with you," cried William. "Oh no!"

"You mean she's still in the marshes?" cried Amanda.

"Well she's not in the cattle truck is she? Look, it's empty!" shouted William, pointing. His nerves felt raw. His heart was pounding. Supposing she's dead, drowned. It will be on my conscience for ever, he thought.

"I thought she'd been dropped off while I was asleep," Amanda said, her face suddenly white.

"You were wrong then."

"Are you going to speak? She's holding on," called Mrs Gaze.

"What am I going to say?" cried William.

"The truth," said Amanda.

"But it's so awful. How could we have left her? How come we didn't stop at her place? What happened?"

"You were worried about Marvin," explained Amanda.

"You mean Dad was," replied William.

"And I could think of nothing but Tango."

"Marvin should have explained. It's his fault,"

shouted William. But he knew that it was really his, his and his father's, because they were responsible. There was no escaping. It was the stark inescapable truth. He remembered his father calling, "All aboard?"

They had all wanted to get home. No one had counted properly.

"William," shouted his mother. "William, are you coming?"

"Yes!" he yelled.

"It's not your fault," Amanda said, touching his arm.

He reacted as though someone had given him an electric shot. "Whose is it then?" he asked, running towards the house. He picked up the phone. His hand was shaking. It seemed oddly detached from his arm, and he wasn't telling it to shake.

"There's been a terrible mistake," he began, "and she's still on the marshes."

His mother was standing listening. Amanda had her face in her hands.

"What do you mean?" demanded Mrs Carruthers in a sharp voice.

"Mean?" asked William. "What I mean is that we thought she was with us, but she wasn't."

There seemed a long silence, one of the longest silences in William's life. He could hear the clock ticking and his mother shouting, "Dad. Dad, come in here . . . " And Amanda wailing, "How could we?" And a cat purring.

"She's alone then, on the marshes," said Mrs Carruthers at last, as though she wanted to be quite certain. "And there's no one with her, she's quite alone."

"There's Rainbow," said William, feeling quite sick.

"Her horse?"

"Yes." They were both trying to gain time, to get over the shock. He was as shocked as she was.

"I'll go in my car. It's dark of course," said Mrs Carruthers, as though she was making up her mind.

"We're going too. We're taking the truck now. We'll stay out all night if necessary. We won't give up," cried William.

He could hear his father now talking in an undertone to Amanda.

"I don't know where it is, where to go," said Mrs Carruthers.

"Tell her we'll meet her at the crossroads," said Mr Gaze. "Tell her we'll be there in ten minutes."

William relayed the message. His mother was already getting food and blankets together, muttering, "Poor girl! How could you forget her, George?"

His father was walking up and down in his dirty boots as though he was lost.

"Ten minutes then," finished William.

"It's so dark, and the sea's coming in. There's floods. It's on the radio," answered Mrs Carruthers.

William put down the telephone.

"I'm coming, I'll just phone my mother," Amanda said.

"You don't have to," replied William, but she was already dialling the number. "She's engaged," she said a second later, putting down the phone.

William's mother handed him a bag full of thermos flasks.

"I'll listen for the phone then. What about telling the police?" she asked.

"We'll see when we get there," replied Mr Gaze. Outside it was raining again. None of them felt like speaking.

"We put the animals first," said William, thinking of Tango. "We shouldn't have done it."

"We're all mad," answered Amanda. "We must be, to leave her behind. Why did Mum have to be engaged?"

No one answered her. They put up the ramp in horrified silence.

"Go back and get the torch out of the scullery, William," said Mr Gaze.

"If only Marvin hadn't had asthma, they would have stayed together," Amanda said.

"It's always, if only," replied William, returning from the house with the torch.

They climbed into the cab. "Supposing she isn't anywhere?" asked Amanda.

"We are going to stay until we find her – dead or alive," replied William.

It was a dark wet night, a night without any hope in it. Mrs Carruthers was waiting at the crossroads in a battered sports car.

"You go with her, William," said Mr Gaze.

"But I don't know her."

"Go with her."

He got out with shaky legs. "I'll show you the way," he said.

She was wearing a shiny raincoat and a woolly cap. "Get in then," she said.

They followed the cattle truck. There wasn't anything to say besides, "What a night!"

Mrs Carruthers looked tense with fear. "How

could it happen?" she asked at last.

"I don't know. We were just so tired," answered William.

"Weren't the police there?"

"They came back to check, but we thought she was in the truck by then. Dad wasn't there when Marvin loaded. He thought she was with him. We all did, but he was too ill to explain. He has asthma. It's a very bad attack," explained William. Mrs Carruthers lit a cigarette. Her hand was shaking. "It was just a chapter of accidents then?" she said.

It was a long way. They both longed for the journey to be over. Wiliam wasn't tired any more. He had reached the point of exhaustion and passed it. He was livng on his reserves now.

"She shouldn't have gone. She didn't have to," said Mrs Carruthers. "Did she go as far as the sea?"

"Yes."

"Alone?"

"I don't know. She was meant to go with Marvin. We were quite nearby. They were meant to go together and then come back to us, but we never saw them again until we got to the truck and saw Marvin," explained William.

"You know there's floods, that the sea has broken through?" asked Mrs Carruthers.

"Yes."He wished time would pass faster, that the cattle truck would go at ninety miles an hour. Sometimes it hardly seemed to move, and after twenty miles it had to stop for petrol.

Mrs Carruthers filled up too. "You never know how many miles we may have to go before the night is over," she said.

"I'm sorry," said William. "I feel so guilty."

"It can't be helped now," said Mrs Carruthers in a voice which belied her words.

"Poor William," said Amanda, sitting in the cab with Mr Gaze. "It must be awful for him being with Mrs Carruthers."

"It's awful for all of us," said Mr Gaze, "but the night's still young, it's barely six o'clock, though it feels much later, seeing we got up so early. And we're nearly there now."

Amanda shut her eyes, silently praying, "God, make her be there. Please God!" And when she opened them, she could see the bunker in the distance, a forgotten relic of another age, small and dumpy in the pouring rain.

Chapter Eight

"Maggy?"

Alison had no idea how long she had lain clutching Maggy. It could have been two minutes or half an hour. She came to with rain beating on her back and twilight all around. She stood up and picked up Maggy, who seemed to have fallen asleep. There was no sign of Rainbow.

"We are going to Granny," Alison said tucking Maggy's poor muddy feet inside her own waterproof.

She could see lights in the distance and they gave her hope. They had reached the last lap of the journey. It was sad about Rainbow, but now Maggy had to come first, decided Alison, because if she didn't have warmth and food she would die. Alison could feel Maggy's heart beating against her side as she walked, and sometimes it was no more than a flutter. Her own boots were clogged with mud and there was water everywhere, but it was rain water now, not water flowing from the sea. Alison rocked Maggy as she walked, hoping for some response, but there was none, and nothing seemed to move besides herself and the falling rain. She was covered with mud, her hands, her face, everything. She couldn't help wondering what the rest of the Patrol were doing now, and how they had come to leave her behind. And then she saw lights quite near, and she started to run. It must be houses she thought, we're saved.

The first house was a bungalow with crazy paving leading to an ornate front door. The bell was the ding-dong sort and there were draped muslin curtains at the windows. A woman answered her ring, speaking through the letter box, "Who is it? Who's there?" she demanded in a scared voice.

"Only me. I've found the lost child," cried Alison. "She's very, very cold. Please can I use your phone? It's urgent."

"I've never heard of a lost child, and I never open the door to strangers. It's not safe, not with things as they are," the woman answered. "Try elsewhere." Alison could hear her feet padding away across fitted carpets, and she shouted, "Please. It's a matter of life and death. Don't you believe me? Do I sound like a robber?" And then she rang the doorbell again, screaming, "People like you deserve to go to hell."

After that she picked up Maggy, saying, "Never mind, darling, there are other houses," and she went back down the path and out into the road again. The next house was a bungalow too, with a dog which barked but this time Alison didn't stop to look for a bell, but banged on the door screaming, "Help me, please. Help! This is an emergency."

A thin man wearing spectacles opened the door a crack and said, "What is it – a crash or something?"

Alison was emotionally exhausted now. "I've

been lost on the marshes. I need a phone. Please can I use yours?" she asked.

"And supposing I haven't one?"

"I've seen the wires. Please."

"Come in then, but take off your boots. I don't want the carpets soiled," he said. "And mind the walls. What are you then – a gypsy?"

Alison put down Maggy to take off her boots.

"She's the lost child. I think she's dying," she said. Everything was beginning to go round and round. She had to reach the phone. Her boots were off now but the ceiling was spinning. And then suddenly the man came to life. He stared at Maggy and shouted, "Maud, come quickly, it's the lost child. She's here!" He ran to the phone, dialled 999, and reported, "We've got the lost child here." And Alison knew that they had made it, that they were home and dry, and that now the grown ups would take over.

"And who are you?" asked the man, still holding the phone.

"Just say I'm part of the Pony Patrol," replied Alison.

The ceiling had stopped spinning now, and the woman had taken hold of Maggy. She was thin too, in a flowery pinny and bedroom slippers. She massaged the child's feet, saying, "Poor little kid. Poor mite. What's happened then? Where's Mummy, then?" and rocked her in her arms.

Maggy twitched and opened her eyes a little and moved her hands. And the woman said, "Get a towel, Sid, and a rug. She's half dead, poor mite."

Alison stood on aching legs, worrying about Rainbow, until the man said, "Come into the

kitchen, it's warmer there. I'll just get a rug and some towels."

Alison sat down, while the woman washed Maggy's feet and the man made tea. Maggy opened her eyes again and looked at her, and the woman said, "She's had almost nothing on, poor kid. She could have died." As if we didn't know, thought Alison.

Police were coming, lights flashing, with an ambulance close behind. They heard the tyres squealing outside on the road. "They didn't take long," the man said.

Maggy was wrapped in a blanket by this time and there was mud all over the kitchen. then the police rushed in accompanied by an old woman with a scarf over her head and glasses. "I'm her Gran," she said. "Maggy, it's me. Gran. How are you, darling?"

Ambulance men put Maggy on a stretcher and someone said, "What about you?" to Alison. "You're the heroine."

Alison said, "I've still got a job to do. I've lost my horse."

Someone said, "You can't search on a night like this." And she said, "I've got to." And then she started to remember the sea water, and the shack and the horses standing outside behind the wire fences. And she said, "There's something else still to be done; there's an old lady in a shack and she's drowning." She had a mug of warm tea in her hands by this time, but suddenly she felt like fainting; luckily one of the policmen caught her before she fell. "Take it easy, Alison. Put your head between your knees," he said. And then "Is there any brandy around, ma'am? I think she could do with a drop."

The brandy stung Alison's throat, but it brought

strength back. She sat in a chair and told them about the shack and the old lady and her animals, who were drowning. She said, "My horse may have gone back to them, he's silly enough," and then she told them how she'd found Maggy. A policeman took down everything she said and he kept smiling and saying, "Well done!" And the day seemed to have lasted for a thousand years already.

The others had nearly reached the bunker now. Rain was falling in torrents. Another five minutes and Mrs Carruthers' car started spluttering, and then stopped altogether.

William put his hand on the horn, opened a window and screamed, "Wait for us, Dad. Stop! We've broken down."

Mrs Carruthers put her face in her hands. "I want Alison," she wailed. "What's she doing out on a night like this? How could you have left her? How could you? She may be dead – drowned. Oh my God!"

And a minute later, Amanda banged on the car window yelling, "What's happened?"

"Distributor's flooded," answered William. "We'd better go on with you."

He opened the door on the other side for Mrs Carruthers. The rain lashed their faces, the wind howled.

"It's like the end of the world, isn't it?" muttered Amanda.

There was no heater in the cattle truck and Mrs Carruthers was shivering.

"Tea? Coffee?" offered William.

She shook her head. "I can't touch a thing with Alison out there," she said.

Everything looked black and sodden and without hope. Amanda thought of Tango, warm and dry, munching hay, safe at last. She should have been rejoicing, but how could she now?

William thought of his own guilt, how no one would ever trust him again and how he should give up the leadership of the Pony Patrol. None of them spoke, because suddenly they were all tired or frightened beyond words.

Then Mrs Carruthers said, "The little girl will be dead of course. She *must* be, lying out there. I'm a nurse and I know." (As if they doubted her) "So it's only Alison who counts now."

William said, "Yes," and imagined her lying somewhere with the sea lapping over her face.

"And Rainbow," added Amanda.

They were off the road now, bumping along the tarmac which ended at the old bunker. William strained his ears, praying, hoping that in a minute he would see Alison waiting with Rainbow, wet and furious, but still alive. Amanda didn't dare look, she was too afraid that Alison wouldn't be there, that they would then have to climb out into the wind and the rain and search the marshes, and she wasn't sure that she had the necessary strength left. But suddenly they all yelled together, "Ambulance, look!" And Mrs Carruthers cried, "Wait. I'm going with her. Stop it! Stop it!" Mr Gaze put his hand on the horn and kept it there. But the ambulance simply put its siren on and rushed past in a great swish of water, while Mrs Carruthers cried, "Oh my God! She could be dead inside."

But the others had seen the police cars now. Mr Gaze stopped the cattle truck and they stared at the bungalow which was ablaze with lights. Then Amanda cried, "Come on, what are we waiting for?" and she and William leapt out of the cab while Mr Gaze stayed to help Mrs Carruthers climb down.

William pushed the bungalow door open and shouted, "Alison! It's all right, Mrs Carruthers, she's here." And Alison cried, "Thank God you've come. I've lost Rainbow. He bucked me off and disappeared. I couldn't follow because of Maggy."

"Maggy?" asked Amanda.

"Yes, the little girl. She's in hospital now. She went in an ambulance."

Alison's head had started to spin again. Her mother had appeared, and Mr Gaze, and everybody seemed to be talking at once, asking questions. When there was silence at last, she said, "There's still a job to be done. That awful shack is under water. We've got to do something about the horses. The Social Services will do something about the old lady, but the animals will drown to death."

"I've got the truck outside. It will take six or seven with some of the partitions down," replied Mr Gaze.

"There's Rainbow too," said William.

"And all those dogs and cats. What about them?" cried Amanda.

"We've already got on to the R.S.P.C.A.," said one of the policemen. "They are sending two inspectors out with animal-catching equipment and a humane killer. Do you think any of the animals are worth saving?"

"Yes," cried Amanda firmly. "At least three horses."

"We must see what shape the old lady is in.

We've got two Landrovers coming in and an ambulance if needed, though it won't be able to go the whole way," the policman continued.

The owners of the bungalow were giving everyone tea and biscuits, apologizing for not having anything else. Alison could feel her strength coming back.

Mr Gaze and the policeman were talking, making plans.

"Is Maggy all right, really all right?" Amanda asked.

Alison nodded. "The Patrol found her in the end," she answered.

"You mean you did," replied William.

"I'm part of the Patrol if you'll have me," she said.

Lights were coming down the road now, Landrovers, an ambulance, men in uniform and waders.

"I'm coming," said Alison.

"You can't," said her mother. "Please."

"I've got to find Rainbow. Besides I may be needed. We've got to bring back the horses."

"Bring back the horses?"

"To the truck. They can't ride in ambulances and Landrovers," she said, laughing.

"You're a heroine," announced Amanda.

"If anyone says that again I'll scream. Why did you leave me behind anyway?" Alison asked.

"It's a long story," replied William.

They climbed into the Landrover. The R.S.P.C.A. inspectors were large jolly men who cracked jokes. Alison wanted them to be serious, to know the misery which lay ahead.

One of the Landrovers was larger than the others

and carried a nurse and a stretcher and breathing equipment.

"Tell us about Maggy?" asked Amanda.

"She's sweet and cuddly and doesn't really talk. She was very, very cold and lying down a cliff. It wasn't funny," Alison replied. "I'll tell you more tomorrow."

The Landrovers were in four-wheel drive already; their wheels were spinning and there seemed nothing around but a great sea of water. There were no lights anywhere and the rain was still falling, relentlessly. Alison strained her eyes, searching for Rainbow. William thought how lovely it would be when everything was accomplished, when they could go home and be warm again and sleep and sleep. Amanda thought, I hope we can save them all, poor horses, they need some happiness after so much hell.

A mile behind them now, pressmen from newspapers had turned up to interview Alison. Since she wasn't there, they had to be content with her mother instead.

"No, I wouldn't call her a quiet girl," Mrs Carruthers was saying. "She's always had plenty of go. No, no boy friends yet. Yes, she's always had courage, you have to have that to ride, don't you? And she has over a hundred rosettes in her bedroom . . ."

Meanwhile the Landrovers had stuck altogether and someone was talking about boats, but William, Alison and Amanda were out in the rain now, shouting, "We'll go on ahead. We've got to find Rainbow," because they were more afraid of finding Rainbow dead, than endangering there own lives. The water was over their boots already.

Their feet squelched in it, but now the police and R.S.P.C.A. inspectors were following with lights and in the distance they could hear barking and then a piercing solitary neigh.

Amanda's mother was telephoning Mrs Gaze again.

"I want my daughter. Where is she?" she demanded.

"Didn't she phone you? She came in and went out again. Poor little Alison got left behind. It's a bit of a crisis really," replied Mrs Gaze, in her calm country voice. "Not to worry."

"I don't know Alison, Mrs Gaze. She doesn't concern me. I want my daughter, Mrs Gaze."

"You'll have to go to the marshes then," said Mrs Gaze, putting down the phone.

Chapter Nine

"He's so cold"

Amanda and Alison weren't afraid any more. It was impossible to be afraid with the police behind you and an ambulance standing by. It was simply a matter of enduring now, of putting one weary, heavy, rain-sodden foot in front of the other, of enduring the cold which seemed to eat into your bones and the wind which turned your face into raw, red, freezing sandpaper.

Alison tripped and nearly fell time after time. It was as though her legs would no longer obey her brain. But the thought of Rainbow kept her going. She knew she couldn't sleep or rest until he was found, and if he was never found she would never have another horse. William was beyond thought. His legs worked automatically, while his hands and feet froze. Amanda was thinking of Tango. Would she ever be fit again? Would she be strong enough to jump next summer? Would she survive?

Mr Gaze had stopped at the water. "I can't go on. I've got arthritis," he said. His bones were aching, his knees creaked, his hips had ceased to move; in the cold and the wet they seemed to have turned solid.

The police had great powerful lights. Their waders kept them dry. And now at last they could see the shack and the side of a horse lying in the water beyond the wire fences. Rainbow was standing thigh deep in water, his broken reins dangling, his saddle lop-sided

Alison started to run then, which made William yell, "Don't, you're splashing all of us and you'll be exhausted in two minutes. Just plod on, it's the only way."

He plodded as though he was following a plough, reserving his energy because it had to last for hours yet, as his ancestors had in years past when they had worked from dawn to dusk.

There was no smoke coming from the shack, no cats now at the window, just the barking dogs.

"Cat's don't like water. They can't swim," said William to no one in particular.

The police and the R.S.P.C.A. inspectors were talking. Two policeman started to knock on the front door, water reaching to their knees. There was no answer.

The children turned towards the fields; there was one horse dead already. A pony foal stood neck high in water. The strongest horses had bagged the highest ground.

"There are halters in the house," William said.

Alison caught Rainbow. Amanda started crying.

"They're in the lobby under the bed," William said. No one seemed to be listening. The horses hadn't moved. It was as though they had lost all hope.

"The water is still rising," said William.

The police were bringing the old lady out on a stretcher. For a moment they thought she was dead; then she looked straight at William and said, "They're taking me away. Look after the horses, boy." And suddenly he could have cried with relief. He started to splash towards the house then, crying, "Come on, what are you two waiting for? You heard what she said – I'm to look after the horses.

The shack was ankle deep in water. An R.S.P.C.A. inspector was counting the cats. William went down on all fours to look under the bed. There was a terrible smell. He found three halters and two more in the lobby. His hands were dripping with water now and his head was swimming.

"There are seven altogether," Amanda said, "not counting the one lying down."

They splashed through water, while the mud below sucked at their boots.

"She said I was to look after the horses," shouted William, "The policemen heard."

Amanda put a halter over a pair of thin grey ears. William caught the foal. Alison gave Rainbow to a policeman to hold and caught a bay carthorse with a white streak down his face. William gave the foal to Alison to hold and slipped the halter over a fine thoroughbred head which was shaking uncontrollably with cold.

"We are taking you home," he said.

An R.S.P.C.A. inspector destroyed the horse lying down with a thud which failed to make the other horses move.

Amanda put the last halter on a small dun pony with a broad forehead and sunken eyes; the eyes set her crying again.

"The others must follow," William said.

"I'll ride Rainbow and lead two," suggested Alison. She could hardly stand now. A policeman held Rainbow while she mounted. "We'll lead some," he said.

An R.S.P.C.A. inspector was asking for a boat with an engine to transport the dogs and cats. "We can't carry them all and you can't expect them to swim," he said. "And there are the chickens too."

William was leading away the thoroughbred wondering what he was called. Marmaduke, Maple Leaf . . . ? Something beginning with M. Amanda had already named the grey Dobbin in her mind and the dun Buttercup. They were a sad procession. The horses lagged and had to be beaten from behind, and the children's hands and feet were beginning to freeze. Alison's teeth wouldn't stop chattering and Amanda felt in a daze, and William was saying to himself over and over again, "Keep right on to the end of the road. Keep right on to the end." He couldn't feel his feet or his hands any more.

The policemen kept encouraging them and suddenly they could see the lights of the cattle truck in the distance. The water ended and there was just solid, heavy exhausting mud stretching as far as the eye could see. Then the police took over the horses and they were told to go in the Landrovers, their hands aching as they returned to life. Mr Gaze was waiting by the cattle truck.

"Eight, is it?" he said, peering into the dark. "I can't take that number."

"You'll have to," cried William, getting out of the Landrover like an old man. "We can't leave any behind. The old lady told me to look after them, and I'm going to."

His eyes were red rimmed, with his eyelids hanging heavy like curtains above them.

"One's only a foal," said Amanda. "And they're all so cold."

"No partitions then. We'll have to come back for them tomorrow. If we pack them tight enough they can't kick, but it's against the law, of course," said Mr Gaze.

The horses were nearly there now. From somewhere the rescuers found the strength to take out the partitions and lean them against a fence.

Amanda thought of Tango. Was she still alive, lying comfortably asleep? Did she know she had come home? To William's home, but home just the same.

Two policemen were carrying the foal now. She was too weak to kick. She was soaked through like a half-drowned animal.

"We'll pen her up in a corner," said Mr Gaze, dragging a partition back up the ramp.

The children stood and watched, too tired to do any more.

"We'll put them in the old straw yard; they'll be all right there," said Mr Gaze, as though talking to himself.

The horses didn't protest or argue; they staggered up the ramp and stood exhausted, their sides heaving.

"We'll stand by their heads," William said.

"Bang on the sides if anything goes wrong," replied Mr Gaze.

Rainbow was loaded last; he tossed his head and rushed inside. He knew he was going home. The bay thoroughbred was still shivering. His skin lay loose over his protruding ribs, his head looked too large for his thin sagging neck and his ears looked like donkey ears above his sunken eyes.

"I think they'll all die," said Amanda suddenly.

"Shut up," yelled William, because he was thinking the same thing. The ramp was thrown up. Then they heard Alison's mother saying, "I want my daughter."

And Alison yelled rudely, "Well you can't have her. She's got a job to do," and her voice was shaking with a mixture of exhaustion and emotion.

And now they were moving, slowly, carefully, because Mr Gaze knew that there wasn't one horse which wasn't exhausted. William thanked God for a father who would always understand.

"I expect the old lady is all scrubbed clean by now," said Amanda. "I bet she hates hospital."

"She had to go," replied William, remembering her eyes looking at him with so much faith, as though she knew she could trust him before all others.

"She must be mad. Couldn't she see that the animals were starving?" replied Alison.

"She wanted to save them from being slaughtered," said William.

The foal was lying still, but her eyes were open. She'll recover, she's young, thought William. We'll have the vet in the morning to listen to the thoroughbred's breathing, if he survives the night. He thought of the vet's bills coming in and every injection costing a fiver and suddenly he saw for the first time what he was taking on.

Amanda must have read his thoughts for she said, "The Patrol will help. We'll raise money to pay for them, won't we, Alison?"

But Alison had fallen asleep standing up and didn't answer.

The carthorse hung his lower lip and shut his eyes and the dun pony looked anxious and stood with quarters hunched listening to the rain outside, and slowly time passed and the miles disappeared under the wheels of the cattle truck, until at last, peering through the slats, William could see familiar trees and smell the scent of home.

"I'll come every day and help," said Amanda. "And we'll pay for Tango to be with you, whatever Dad says."

"I wonder which will die. I think he'll be the first," said William, pointing at the thoroughbred. "I wonder what he's called – all their names begin with M."

"None of them will die," said Amanda. "We won't let them."

"I wish I had a rug for him, he's so cold," said William. They stopped to drop Alison. Her mother was waiting, talking about hot drinks and hot baths. Rainbow rushed down the ramp, his coat steaming. Alison could hardly stagger. "See you," she said.

There were men waiting to take photographs, asking questions. Then the ramp was thrown up again and they were moving once more.

Then at last they reached the farm and Pete, the farm hand, was there waiting with a lantern, and Amanda's mother was shrieking, "Come home at once, you naughty girl." And Mrs Gaze, in her apron and gum boots, was saying, "Oh, the poor animals. They look half drowned."

Mr Gaze backed the truck into the old straw yard which was roofed over and enclosed on three sides with a small yard in the middle.

"Bed it down with straw, Pete," he said.

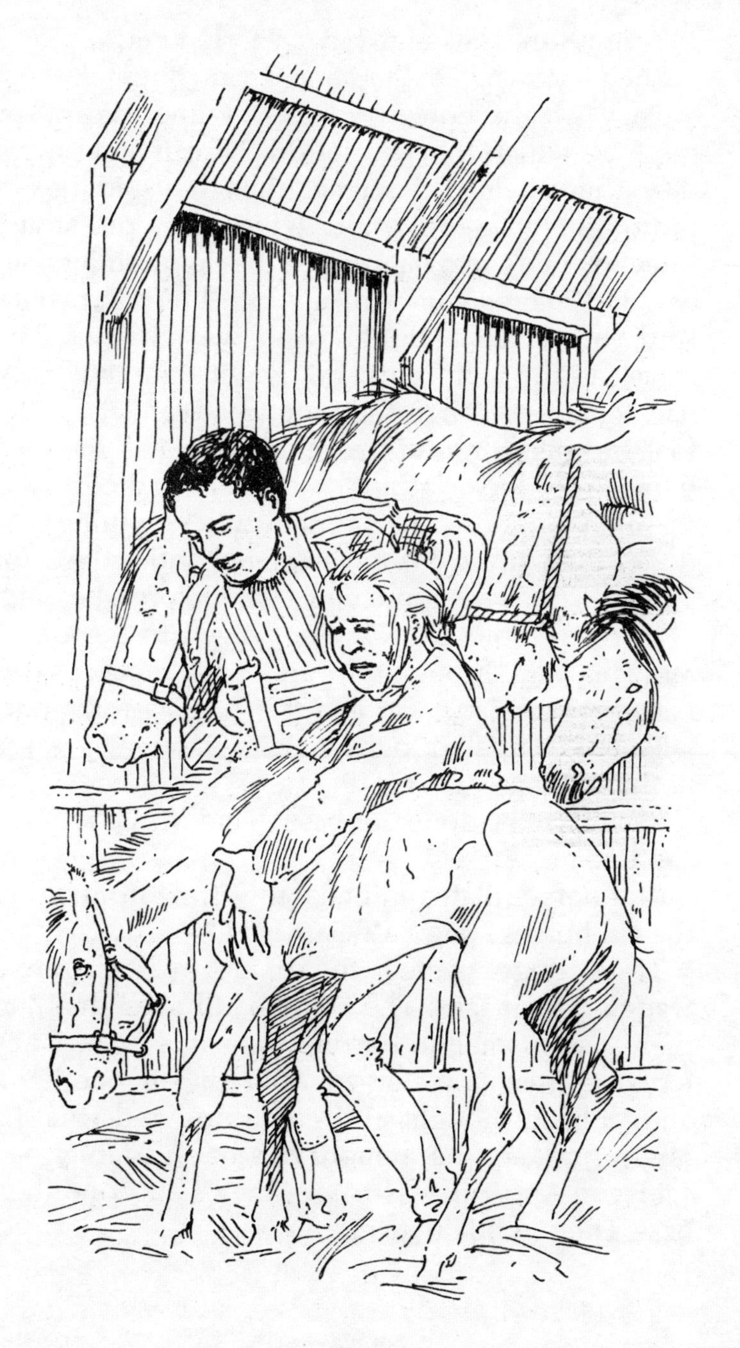

"We've only got a ton left," retorted Pete.

"Bed it down, just the same."

They led the horses out one by one, except for the foal, which they carried to the calf shed more dead than alive. They fetched them hay and the old thoroughbred a rug, under which they put straw. They fetched them oats which they poured into old wooden mangers and mixed with bran and chaff. And they filled a trough with water, while Mrs Gaze fed the foal from a bottle with the milk they had for calves. Then they found a blanket for the foal and tied it round her middle. And all the time they hardly spoke because they were so tired.

Amanda ignored her mother till everything was done, then she went to the stable and looked for Tango who was munching hay, before she said, "I'm ready now, Mum." She waved to the Gazes and splashed through the yard to her mother's car. Her feet were still wet and her hair was like rats' tails, but compared to the state of the horses it was nothing.

"Well, we've done our best," said Mr Gaze. "We can't do more."

"I'll pop out later and take the straw from under the old horses's rug," William said.

Their dogs waited for them in the porch, wagging their tails. The kettle had boiled dry, and there was a smell of burning from the oven. They took off their boots slowly, blinking in the light, and William thought of the morning and what he might find, and he thought of what his father had said and knew it was true – they had done their best. They could do no more.

Chapter Ten

"All heroes now"

William could hear the church bells ringing and knew he had overslept. Yesterday seemed like a dream now, yet he knew it had happened. He fell out of bed, pulled on clothes. A watery sun shone on the window panes of his room which was at the top of the old farmhouse, so that the music he so often played full blast troubled no one. He bumped his head as he hurtled down the attic stairs. He ached all over and his throat was sore.

"Why didn't you call me, Mum?" he yelled. "I wanted to be up first. I wanted to see the horses –"

"The vet's just come," she called from the kitchen.

"You should have called me. I wanted to be first." He rushed outside into the yard. The vet was bending over the thoroughbred saying, "He's old. He's had a long innings."

"Give him a chance," answered William. "He still belongs to the old lady. You can't put him down without her permission." He hated his father for not waiting. They were his responsibility, not his father's.

"Your Mum wanted you to sleep on. You

wouldn't wake up," his father said. The foal was standing up; the other horses munched hay steadily as though they would never stop.

"I'll come back tomorrow then," the vet said. "I'll just give him a couple of injections before I go."

William knew what they would be – an antibiotic to help the old horse's chest and Vitamin B to pep him up.

He could see Amanda bicycling into the yard now, calling, "I'm sorry I'm late. I never heard the alarm clock."

She looked clean and tidy, while William felt scruffy and knew his hair was on end. She went to look at Tango first, then the foal.

"They all need names," she said.

The vet put away his needle and put the horse's rug back into place. "He's only got a fifty-fifty chance," he said. "Give him glucose in his water and a damp feed with treacle or molasses in it. By the way, someone gave me a bag of nuts for you. You were on the local news at eight o'clock this morning; there was an appeal for food for the horses."

"What are you talking about?" demanded Amanda.

"There was a piece about your Patrol and the little girl and the horses. It was very complimentary." He went to his car and heaved out a bag of pony cubes. "I called on Miss Bates before I came here. They're from her," he said.

"Oh well, thank you very much," William said. "They are going to cost a lot of money to feed, so every bit helps."

"You did very well. You all deserve medals.

Here's some powder to kill the lice," the vet said. "I should use it as soon as possible."

"I can't believe it really happened," said Amanda, after the vet had gone. "How did we fit so much into yesterday? How could so much happen in a single day? How did we walk so far? It's like a dream now; all that agony. I have to keep looking at the horses here to know it's true. How could we find Tango and the little girl and all these horses in one day? It just doesn't seem possible."

"Well, Alison found the girl," answered William.

"But then we had to find Alison. It seems crazy really. I mean most days are so dull nothing happens at all. Why did it all happen yesterday?"

"We got up very early, and we stayed up very late," replied William. "If we did that every day, more might happen. As it is we waste at least a third of our lives in sleep. Come on, let's muck out the stables."

His father was mixing a mash for the thoroughbred. Mulberry was standing, run up like a greyhound, in his box. His legs were filled round the fetlock and he looked stiff all over. Tango looked fatter already. She pricked her ears and whinnied when she saw Amanda.

"She knows me. I knew she would," Amanda said. "Dad's moving out of her loosebox. He's being terribly kind. I can take her home tomorrow, if it's all right with you."

"Of course. Anything you say," replied William, remembering that he had had no breakfast.

"Who's going to pay for all this, that's what I want to know," said Mr Gaze, giving the foal some mash.

"We'll hold a jumble sale, a coffee morning, we'll think of something," Amanda said.

"You went to find a little girl and came back with this lot – it takes some explaining, doesn't it?" asked Mr Gaze, laughing.

"We'll de-louse them tomorrow," said William. "It's a terrible job but it must be done."

Alison was awake, sitting up, trying to find the energy to get up. Her mother was just going out. She stopped to stick a thermometer in Alison's mouth. "Shut your mouth, but don't swallow it," she said.

"What about Rainbow?" cried Alison.

"Don't talk. He's all right," said Mrs Carruthers, taking her pulse.

The rain had stopped at last. A watery sun shone on the window panes. Yesterday seemed like a nightmare without beginning or end. Was it all true? Did she really bring the horses through the floods? Alison wasn't sure now.

"There's a bit about you in the paper, 'Little girl found by girl on horse'," quoted her mother. "Just as I thought. You *have* got a temperature and you are wheezing too. I'll have to ring Dr Austin."

"But it's Sunday," wailed Alison, beginning to cough.

"We can't help that."

"And what about Rainbow?"

"He's all right. I'm quite capable of looking after him."

"But you can't muck him out."

"He can be deep litter then. He's got hay and water, and he's had some pony cubes and I'll put him out presently. I had a pony when I was a child. I'm not an imbecile," her mother said.

I wanted to see the horses. Some may be dead by

now. Why did I oversleep? thought Alison. I'm missing everything. She could hear her mother talking downstairs now, saying, "Yes, a touch of pneumonia I should say." Doctor Austin always took her seriously because she was a nurse. He would come straight away, running up the stairs. Alison lay back on her pillows and fell asleep again, and dreamt that she was marrying William in a great cathedral and that her father had come back to give her away.

Marvin was well again. He got out of bed and he wasn't wheezing any more. "I'm all right, Mum," he yelled. "It's passed off. Have you fed Skinflint?"

He rushed down to the stable. Skinflint was brushed, cleaned, rugged and bandaged; the stable was mucked out with the straw banked high round the sides. However hard he tried, when Marvin mucked out, the stable never looked as good. He rushed indoors again. Being well after asthma gave him the same feeling as a holiday from school – a feeling that he had escaped from something nasty.

It was eleven o'clock. The sun shone through bare branches outside; the crazy-paving paths were washed clean by the night's rain.

"I'll ring up Amanda," he cried.

Her mother answered. "It's a very long story, Marvin. I think you had better jump on your bike and go down to the farm. Amanda's there. The little girl is found, Alison found her. It's in the paper. You are all heroes now," she said.

"Where was the little girl?" asked Marvin.

"Somewhere by the sea." He felt let down suddenly. I should have been there. I should have fought off this asthma somehow, he thought. He put down the receiver. "I'm going to the farm," he yelled.

"But you haven't had any breakfast," complained his mother.

"I don't care." He had to pump up his back tyre. His father was weeding the drive. Skinflint whinnied from the stable. I've missed everything, thought Marvin. Alison will have all the glory now. I let her down. I let everyone down. He couldn't remember much of the evening before, only being sick and a terrible dizziness, and Skinflint carrying him through mud.

When he reached the farm he could see nothing but strange horses. Amanda and William were mucking out boxes.

"Hurray! here comes another helper," yelled William. Marvin went to the straw yard. "Who are these?" he asked. "Should I recognize them?"

"You might. They are the old lady's. We rescued them," said Amanda.

"I don't remember doing it."

"You didn't, you weren't there."

Three children were coming up the drive now, carrying bags. We've brought some carrots for the horses. We heard about them on the local news," they said.

William dealt with them, while Amanda told Marvin what had happened, mucking out as she talked, humping sacks of shavings from box to box.

"I missed it all, then," he said, when she had finished.

"You couldn't help it, you were ill. You can make up for it now, because there are all these dreadful skeletons to look after and it's school tomorrow, and no one knows how we will pay the bills for

them. The farm isn't run as a charity and the vet's bills are going to be enormous," Amanda said. "Worm doses alone will cost nearly sixty pounds, and then their teeth are sure to need rasping and that will cost another fifty. And they are all having oats and mashes and hay."

"What a problem! But it will costs hundreds," moaned Marvin.

"Exactly," agreed Amanda.

The three children were leaving now and the looseboxes were clean.

"Now for the de-lousing," William said.

"I can't help because of my asthma," replied Marvin. "I'm sorry."

William gave Amanda an old coat to wear. They worked quickly paying special attention to the tops and tails and around the ears. When they had finished William said, "Let's go in and change. There might be some bread and cheese around, or some freshly baked cakes. You never know . . ."

"They're going to cost a mass to feed," said Marvin looking at the horses in the straw yard. "That grey looks like a walking toast rack."

"He whinnies all the time. He's sweet," William said. "It's the old thoroughbred which is between life and death. The vet has been once and he's coming again tomorrow."

Marvin sighed. "You were a fool to take them on," he said.

"Right again," replied William laughing.

"It will ruin your father; it's not as though you're rich," continued Marvin, following William into the shabby old farmhouse. "I mean, just look at your car, it won't pass another M.O.T test will it? Any fool can see that."

"Do stop being so pessimistic," said Amanda.

They drank tea and tried to make plans.

"Seven horses costing ten pounds a week to feed. That's seventy pounds," said Marvin. "And the winter's ahead. It's a long time till spring."

"We need a blacksmith. Their feet are in a terrible condition," said Amanda.

"It's not as though we can hire them out or anything. They are going to need the best of food, right round to the spring. You can't do it, William," said Marvin.

"I can and I will," replied William.

"But how?"

"We can graze them at the roadside," suggested Amanda.

"What? After school? It will be dark in a few days. The clocks are being moved back," replied Marvin.

"I couldn't refuse," said William. "Perhaps we can get some of them in a home for old horses."

"If they *are* old."

"It isn't fair on your father," said Marvin, looking around the kitchen. "He's not a rich man."

Suddenly William saw clearly for the first time what he was taking on. There would be hours of work to do, as well as money to be found. They could hold jumble sales, but would anyone come to support a bunch of old horses?

"I'll think of something. We can find them nice homes when they are better; the foal is better already," he said.

"Who wants a foal at this time of year?" asked Marvin. "And that thoroughbred is going to need pounds and pounds of food. He'll cost a fortune to keep."

Marvin knew deep down inside himself that he was being unfair, that this wasn't the time to raise despair; but he was furious that they had rescued the horses without him, that he had missed everything. William guessed how he felt, but knew too that what he was saying was right, however unpleasant. He knew he couldn't expect his father and mother to bear the cost, but he couldn't see any other way out.

"Something will turn up. It has to," he said.

Chapter Eleven

"A piece of paper"

The thoroughbred was dead the next day.

"We did our best. He died peacefully on a warm bed," said Mr Gaze. "We could do no more."

School seemed to last for ever. William was too bored to listen to the lessons. In the evening the blacksmith came. He spent a long time rasping hoofs and the bill was thirty pounds. William was able to look at the horses properly now. The dun mare was cobby with a kind head and small Welsh ears; the grey was nearly fifteen hands with a well-bred head and a goose rump; the heavy bag horse was clumsy with the feet of a cart horse, a heavy lip and a small eye. There was a plain bay pony with a star and one white sock who seemed to have no good points to him at all – his head was too large, his shoulder straight, his neck ewe, his hocks sickle. And a piebald with high knee action who carried his thin head high, and finally the foal which was blue roan.

It seemed impossible to William, now, that he would ever cope with them all. At school the staff talked about exams incessantly, as though they were the only things which counted in life. They gave him hours of homework to do. And they kept saying. "If you don't work you won't pass next year and then there'll be no work for you – nothing."

Sometimes he wanted to scream, "To hell with exams."

Amanda's parents kept on at her too, forbidding her to go to the farm, saying, "Looking after Tango is enough. Let William look after the others. He took them on, not you." She rang up to apologize, saying, "I'll come tomorrow," but tomorrow it was just the same. The old lady's horses were all coughing now and they had to be kept away from the other animals on the farm. The vet seemed to be there every day, listening to their chests, injecting them with penicillin.

William's father said, "Don't worry, lad. It will all turn out right in the end." But he was looking worried too. Two days passed like this, strange sunlit days when the sky was grey and yellow, and the trees looked stark and beautiful, and then the telephone rang. William was cleaning out the straw yard, knowing that three hours of homework waited indoors. The horses whinnied to him. He had started to give them names, to imagine turning them out. Their coughs were subsiding. If it wasn't for the bills growing all the time he could have felt happy. His photograph had been in the paper along with Alison's, Marvin's and Amanda's – terrible school photographs. And they had had a "write up" in the local paper. In a way they were now famous. Small children still arrived with cut grass, dandelions and carrots for the horses. And a farmer had left a bag of oats for them, but it wasn't enough – just a drop in the ocean of food which was needed, and would go on being needed right round to April next year. The R.S.P.C.A. had rung up. The police had been round to look, but nothing had been decided and now there was a telephone call for William.

"You're wanted at the hospital, William," his mother said.

"What ever for? I'm well, there's nothing wrong with me," cried William.

"It's to see the old lady. She wants to see you. I'll get out the car. Hurry up. It's urgent," called his mother.

He remembered what Marvin had said about the car. It was rusting through, even he could see that now.

"Perhaps she'll tell me their names," he said, getting into the front beside his mother.

"Whose names?"

"The horses', of course."

"They can't stay," said his mother. "You know that. We can't go on keeping them for ever. It's going to kill your father. We can't afford it. We are not a charity. The R.S.P.C.A. should have put them down. It isn't fair."

"I know," he said. "But they can't be put down now when they are getting better."

"And you can't do all the work. You've got your exams next year."

"I'll scream if anyone mentions exams again," he said. He didn't want to see the old lady. Old age frightened him. "Aren't you coming too?" he asked when they reached the hospital.

"They said just you," replied his mother. "I'll read my *Woman's Weekly*. She's in Parker Ward."

Only a few weeks ago he had been in hospital.

He knew what it was like lying there waiting for meals to come – for time to pass. He found Parker Ward, but he had forgotten what the old lady looked like. "I'm William Gaze. I've come to see the old lady from the marshes; the one who nearly drowned," he told a nurse.

He wished he had done his hair and changed his shoes.

"She's by herself in a side ward. Follow me, dear," the nurse said. He wished Amanda had come with him.

She looked frail. There was another lady sitting beside her on a chair. "I'm William Gaze," he said.

The nurse fetched him a chair and puffed up the old lady's pillows. He could see she was different, pale and scrubbed with her hair pinned back. She looked at him with watery eyes. "How are the horses?" she asked.

"The bay died, the big one. We did our best. We had the vet."

"Poor old Marmaduke. I brought him home from Poland twenty years ago. He was pulling a coal cart. He had to go, I expect."

"He just died."

"I've written their names down for you. I hope you can read my writing. I'm not very well. I've made them over to you – all of them. Those you can't find homes for, you must destroy. Is that clear?"

He nodded.

"Quite clear?" She was very weak. "I've had it signed and witnessed. My niece here is looking after the other animals," she said.

He took the piece of paper. "I'll do my best," he answered. He wanted to say something about money, but it didn't seem the right moment.

"I would like the ponies to go to children, nice children," croaked the old lady. "And here's an envelope. Don't open it until this evening, when you go to bed – not before. Is that clear?"

"Yes."

Her eyes were shutting. She looked tired and incredibly old in her white hospital nightgown.

"You had better go," said the niece, standing up. "Thank you for coming. She wanted to see you before she died."

He said "Goodbye", and walked back down a long corridor and outside into sunshine.

He got into the car and said, "She's dying. She gave me their names."

"Is that all?" asked his mother.

"Yes, and instructions. I'm to find them nice homes or have them put down if I can't."

He read out the names. "Maple Leaf, Marmaduke, Misty, Marigold, Old Mac, Messenger, Mermaid, Mrs Mop. Some of them are dead," he said. "I'm going to call a meeting of the Patrol tonight. At least – of Marvin, Alison, Amanda and myself to decide how to keep them. We will raise money, Mum, I promise," he continued, "we'll manage somehow."

"I don't know how," she said, "with the vet coming every day. And sacks of oats going down their throats every week."

"They are getting better. They aren't coughing so much now."

"Can you sell them when they are well?" asked his mother.

"She didn't say so. She said to find them nice homes," replied William.

His mother had always been careful with money.

It was his father who didn't mind spending, who was always saying, "You can't take it with you, lad."

When he reached the farm, he went straight to the old lady's horses. They knew him now. They clustered around him like friends all wanting to be the nearest to him. They trusted him because he had brought them home and they always would trust him now. He put his arms round their necks, whispered in their ears. His father had put the foal in with the others. "You're Misty," he told her, looking at the list. And the cart horse must be Old Mac, he decided, and the grey, Mermaid, the piebald, Messenger. And the dun, Marigold, and the bay could only be Maple Leaf. They all had their own characters. Messenger was always nudging him, while Mermaid stood aloof waiting for him to come to her. There wasn't one which was like another.

"I'm keeping you until you're all well," he told them, before going indoors to ring the other members of the Patrol.

It was nearly dark now. He rang Alison first.

"Of course I'll come. I'm better. The penicillin worked like a miracle. I'm up and Mum can bring me; she'll pick up the others too. It's no bother. I'm dying to see the horses; to see you all in fact. I can't believe it really happened. It seems impossible now; but when I see the horses again, I'll know it's true. Hold on – I'll just speak to Mum," she said.

He waited, biting his nails.

"All fixed," she said, returning. "I'll phone the others. What shall I say?"

"That's it urgent; that I've seen the old lady and she's dying."

"Not really?"

"Yes."

"I knew she would if she was moved. Old ladies are like that. You ask Mum," said Alison.

"She's given me a letter to open later and I'm to find the horses homes. Hurry up and come," he said, putting down the receiver.

He ate tea and did his homework at the same time, spread out across the kitchen table. He didn't understand the maths and the geography was about North America. He had to draw a map and he kept making smudges; if he hadn't been fifteen he would have cried. He was drawing the map for the third time when they arrived.

"We've seen the horses. I hope you didn't mind. The yard light was on and they look marvellous, much, much better," cried Alison. "Mum is coming back for us in twenty minutes, is that all right?"

"Perfect. Would anyone like coffee?" asked William, clearing up his homework.

They shook their heads and he took them upstairs to his room, saying, "Excuse the mess," and hastily cleared books off chairs.

"It's about money-raising," he said when they were all sitting down. "I can't let Dad go on paying the bills, and the vet's will be at least a hundred pounds."

"What did I say? Dad says you're mad. They should be put down. There's not one with any breeding," Marvin said. "If you sent them to a sale they would go for meat; you can't spend all that money on worthless animals – it's simply throwing good money after bad."

"Here are their names on a piece of paper signed by the old lady. She's called Ruth Maudsley. She's given them to me," William said. Alison took the paper.

"Poor you, that's all I say," answered Marvin. "What a nasty piece of paper. You can't even read the writing properly."

"Aren't you being rather mean, Marvin?" asked Amanda.

"Someone has to talk sense. For goodness' sake, who's going to donate money to keep a lot of old horses alive?"

"Me for one," answered Alison.

"What? Sixty pounds a week?"

"We can have a Bring and Buy coffee morning," suggested Alison.

"And who will come?" asked Marvin.

"Lot's of people."

"I can't afford anything because of Tango. She's having injections of Vitamin B, and speical vitamins in her food which cost the earth," said Amanda, "but of course I will help run something."

William went to the window and looked out. Across the yard he could see the horses standing together, warm and comfortable in the moonlight. They weren't coughing any more. In three months they would be well. Tomorrow he planned to start dosing them against worms; one dose wouldn't be enough, they would need another within two months. He knew he couldn't pay the vet's bills and he knew too that only half a dozen people would come to a Bring and Buy coffee morning, because the houses were scattered around the farm – there was no proper village, and people would rather support the victims of earthquakes, than a few old horses. And yet he had promised the old lady.

Amanda was talking again now. "If only the bills weren't so huge," she said. "If there was only one horse to support instead of six."

"Exactly," said Alison. "I'm sure we could raise ten or twenty pounds, but that's like a drop in the ocean when there's six horses to feed."

"I can't have them put down because I've accepted them, can't you see?" cried William. "She wanted the ponies to go to children, nice children. As soon as they stop coughing I can start looking. It's just the bills now. Can't you understand?"

"Misty can't go anywhere. She's too young," said Marvin. "And the cart horse won't do for a child either." He was standing up now as though preparing to leave. Suddenly William hated him.

"I'll count you out, then," he said in a withering voice.

"Please do," said Marvin.

"I'll help, just give me another week to get better," said Alison.

"So will I. But do please remember Tango has to come first," said Amanda. "Let's meet again at the weekend. We'll have more time then. We must be able to think of something."

"Yes we must," agreed Alison.

"You were a fool to accept them – sentimental. I'm surprised. Farmers' sons should have more sense," said Marvin.

William would have liked to kick him down the stairs.

"I'll help, I promise," said Alison. "Really. Truly."

He didn't believe them and they could see it on his face.

They were wrapping scarves round their necks now, preparing to go downstairs. He had lent Amanda a pony, helped her bringing Tango home, and now she was leaving without helping him.

Alison's mother was hooting outside. Alison was coughing again, saying, "I'm sorry. I shall help, honestly, just give me a little time to get well."

And all the time he could see the bills growing, the oats being eaten, the stack of hay growing smaller in the yard. There wasn't time to think, to plan, there was no time to spare.

"I should think next time, before you accept a present," said Marvin. "Personally, I wouldn't be in your shoes for all the world."

"I'll ring you on Friday," said Amanda.

"See you," said Alison.

He shut the door behind them.

"Well?" asked his mother, coming into the hall. "Any bright ideas?"

"No, nothing. Nothing at all," he said.

He felt hot suddenly, and he could feel beads of sweat on his forehead, and he thought I mustn't be ill. There isn't time for illness, not at the moment, not until everything about the horses is settled and "we're out of the wood" as Dad would say. He loved that term, it described everything, he thought, the darkness of wood and the relief when you were outside in the light, when the ordeal was over.

But someone was knocking on the kitchen door now. His mother opened it with a sigh, muttering, "What ever is it now?"

Mrs Carruthers barged her way inside, without

asking permission. "I want a word with you, Mrs Gaze," she said, and William thought, more trouble!

Mrs Gaze seemed to shrink a little. "Go ahead," she said.

"Alison is crying her eyes out in the car and I can't have her upset like this. She is only just getting over pneumonia. If it wasn't for modern antibiotics, she could have died. I shouldn't have brought her, I can see that now," said Mrs Carruthers, looking straight at William (who decided to stare her out). "Please tell your son to leave her alone, Mrs Gaze. Not to telephone or pester her any more. I'm sure you will understand."

"My son is not in the habit of pestering people," replied William's mother.

"I'm glad to hear it," replied Mrs Carruthers, slamming the door after her.

"Whew!" exclaimed William. "Poor Alison."

"You have some strange friends, I must say," replied his mother, looking at him. "And you don't look too well yourself, either."

He sat down at the kitchen table, saying, "I'm sorry. I bring you nothing but trouble, Mum – expense and trouble," and now his teeth were chattering.

"They've let you down, and that's a fact," replied his mother, feeling his forehead. "You're ill as well, so you had better get to bed and I'll bring you up some nice hot soup by and by."

"I'm going to keep the horses, whatever happens," said William. "I promised and it was a death-bed promise, and that's sort of sacred, isn't it?"

"I wouldn't know about that," replied his mother, filling a hot water bottle at the old stone sink in the scullery. "But I *do* know you need a spot of bed."

He climbed the stairs slowly, clutching the hot water bottle to himself. At times his head seemed to be spinning and he kept seeing the old lady in hospital again, so old and clean and fragile, quiet different to the strange independent old lady they had first met at the shack. He felt very cold and very tired and not very hopeful as, with shaking hands, he undressed and climbed into his high, old-fashioned bed. He knew it would be easy to give up now, to simply call the vet and have the horses destroyed, and their remains carted away. All his worries would be over then, except that his conscience would keep saying to him, "You didn't keep your word." And the feeling that he had been false to the horses' trust in him would be there for ever. He would know for the rest of his life that he had let them down in their hour of need, betrayed them for the sake of a quiet life. And I don't want a quiet life, he thought, not really, not deep down inside myself.

Chapter Twelve

"I don't want them put down"

"I *want* William to ring me up, Mummy. I *want* to help. Can't you understand?" shouted Alison as they drove away from the farmhouse.

"Well, I want *you* well," replied her mother. "I can't have you crying day after day over a lot of mangy old horses."

"They aren't mangy," choked Alison. "They just need looking after."

"William took them on, so let William look after them," replied Mrs Carruthers.

Amanda sat in the back, thinking of home, of Tango waiting for her feed and the colour television on in the sitting room. Her mother would be waiting to say, "Take off your shoes. Don't bring mud into the house. Wash your hands," as soon as she stepped inside.

"Amanda and William are the best friends I've ever had," said Alison, after a bout of coughing. "Why should I give up William?"

"Because you've got your exams and your future to think about," replied her mother.

"I don't care about exams and my future. I care about William and the horses," cried Alison.

They were at Amanda's house now. She got out of the car and said, "Thank you for the lift."

Tango was looking over her loosebox door. She wrinkled her nose and nickered. Amanda mixed her a feed, wondering why life was never perfect, why there always had to be a snag somewhere.

In the car Marvin said, "I think William's a bit mad. Those horses aren't worth anything. There isn't one which would be placed in a showing class."

William was in bed now, sitting up sipping soup, while his mother fussed over the room saying, "We can't have it like this if the doctor's coming tomorrow. Why don't you hang up your clothes? And put your dirty socks out to wash?"

His teeth had stopped chattering. He thought, we've succeeded in so many things – we found Tango, Alison found Maggy, we brought out the horses, and saw the old lady to safety. You would think someone would help us, would care. He could hear his father coming upstairs now with steps which made the walls shake. Another minute and he was standing looking at him, still in his outdoor boots

"I don't want the doctor. I'm perfectly all right," William said.

"So you are ill," said his father. "You've brought home all those extra mouths to feed and now you're ill. Well I can't go on doing it all. There's a cow calving tonight, and it's market day tomorrow; I can't work more than twenty hours a day, not with my arthritis."

He looked tired and he smelt of the cowsheds. "They'll have to go," he said. "I can't help your old lady. I can't go on keeping them for nothing; I haven't got the fodder and I can't buy it in for them, I haven't got the money."

He was shaking with fatigue. "Why don't you get your girl friends to help?" he asked.

"They aren't my girl friends. They do their best. Alison's ill and Amanda has Tango to look after," he said.

"Just one horse and we've got six, plus our own, of course," said his father bitterly.

"I'll turn them out tomorrow, I promise. I just want to worm them first, so they don't infest the pastures for our own horses," William said. He felt very weak now. He wondered how he would get up in the morning. How he would manage to dose six horses without any help. He felt as though he was trapped in a pit and there was no way out. His father was hobbling away now, muttering, "Isn't there any supper tonight?"

His mother took the empty soup bowl away. "You'll have to stay in until the doctor comes in the morning," she said.

"I can't. I've got to feed the horses," he said.

"I'm ringing the hospital. I'm telling the old lady we can't cope," said his mother. "That it isn't fair to expect us to. I'm doing it for your good and your father's. She must find someone else to look after her old horses."

"She won't speak to you,"he replied. "There isn't a phone in her room so she can't."

"I shall speak to someone else then," his mother replied. She shut the door behind her, while he cried, "Please don't. Please . . ."

He tried to get out of bed, but now he couldn't stand; and the room spun round and round, and for a moment he couldn't see anything. It was then that he remembered the envelope, which he was to open at bedtime. He had put it in a drawer. He staggered across the room like an old man and got it out. He sat on the bed and looked at it. It was addressed in a faint, crooked handwriting to Master William Gaze. It was sealed with sealing wax. For a time he was afraid to open it, afraid that it might contain more responsibility. Finally however he broke the sealing wax, pulled open the envelope, took out a letter which he couldn't read because the ink was faint and his eyes wouldn't focus any more. Then he took out the rest of the package and looked at it. He read the writing on the notes £100, £50. They were large and thick; he had never seen such notes before. He tipped the envelope out on the bed and stared at the contents. He scooped up the money and then put it down again and thought, it can't be real, while he felt hope rising inside like a tempest blotting out everything else. There were hundreds of pounds lying on his bed now, hundreds and hundreds. His head started whirling with hope. Were they real? he wondered. Were they for the horses? He stumbled to the door, opened it and yelled, "Mum, come here quickly." But she was on her way already, calling, "She's dead. The old lady died five minutes ago, just when I telephoned. I don't know what we can do now," and she was crying.

"Look!' he said from the doorway. "Come and look. Do you think it's real?"

She stared at the notes, then ran to the door to call, "George, come up here a moment – quickly."

"There's a letter too. Can you read it?" asked William. He was back in bed now, staring at the

notes which covered it. His mother stood under the light to read the letter.

This is what she read: "Dear William. This money is for the dear horses. If there's any over when you've found them nice homes, it is for you. My niece fetched it for me from my home. It is for hay and oats and for the vet, if they need one. I know I haven't much longer and I am so glad I met you, because I can tell by your face that you are all right and one of the old breed, and there's not many of them about these days. God bless you and keep you, William. Ruth Maudsley."

"I don't want any for myself," said William.

His father was counting the money now. Three hundred, five hundred, a thousand," he said.

"I shall ring up the others in a minute," William said.

"There's three thousand pounds here," his father exclaimed.

"Enough, anyway, to stop us worrying any more," replied William.

"Who would have thought she had that sort of money in that old shack," said his father.

"She was a good person really," replied William, lying back on his pillows. "Just a bit mad I suppose." He felt as though he had been labouring in a storm for a long time and had come home to rest. He saw the horses growing well, their coats gleaming, their eyes shining. He saw the Patrol riding them, himself getting the younger members to help; then finding them homes.

"I'll feed them once more, just tomorrow morning," his father said. "Just to oblige, after that you can hire yourself some help!"

"The old cart horse will be the hardest to settle,"

William said. "Then the foal. Won't Alison and Amanda be pleased?

His mother was putting the money back into the envelope.

I can even help Amanda with Tango, William thought. I can pay her vet's bills, because the old lady wouldn't mind. If she was alive she would say, "Go on, boy, it's there for the spending" and give one of her great cackling laughs.

The last few days stretched behind him like a half-real nightmare, but we came through in the end, he thought. His mother was fond of saying "If you do what's right, everything will come right in the end". And this time it had happened, the Patrol had been through flood and storm and brought out Maggy and the horses and everything had come right, they were home safe and dry. He shut his eyes and thought, I'm happy, no more worries, no more rows over money; the Patrol goes on and the horses are saved. And it was a wonderful happiness; the kind which comes after suffering and endeavour, like sunshine after a great storm.

PONY PATROL

The Pony Patrol – a team of young riders whose sworn aim is to patrol the countryside on horseback, watching, searching and protecting the peace of the land.

Follow the adventures of the Pony Patrol riders in Christine Pullein-Thompson's gripping series of books.

Pony Patrol	£2.99 ☐
Pony Patrol S.O.S.	£2.99 ☐

Available in 1992:

Pony Patrol Fights Back
Pony Patrol and the Mystery Horse

All Simon & Schuster Young Books are available at your local bookshop or can be ordered direct from the publisher. Just tick the titles you want and fill in the form below. Prices and availability subject to change without notice.

Simon & Schuster Cash Sales Department, PO Box 11, Falmouth, Cornwall, TR10 9EN, England.

Please enclose a cheque or postal order to the value of the cover price and allow the following for postage and packing:
UK: 80p for the first book, and 20p for each additional book ordered up to a maximum charge of £2.00.
BFPO: 80p for the first book, and 20p for each additional book.
OVERSEAS & EIRE: £1.50 for the first book, £1.00 for the second book, and 30p for each subsequent book.

Name ....

Address ....

....

Postcode ....

DRINA

Follow Drina's fortunes, from her first ballet lessons to her triumphant appearances on stages throughout the world, in the popular Drina series of books.

Ballet for Drina	£2.99 ☐
Drina's Dancing Year	£2.99 ☐
Drina Dances in Exile	£2.99 ☐
Drina Dances in Italy	£2.99 ☐
Drina Dances Again	£2.99 ☐
Drina Dances in New York	£2.99 ☐
Drina Dances in Paris	£2.99 ☐
Drina Dances in Madeira	£2.99 ☐
Drina Dances in Switzerland	£2.99 ☐
Drina Goes on Tour	£2.99 ☐
Drina, Ballerina	£2.99 ☐

All Simon & Schuster Young Books are available at your local bookshop or can be ordered direct from the publisher. Just tick the titles you want and fill in the form below. Prices and availability subject to change without notice.

Simon & Schuster Cash Sales Department, PO Box 11, Falmouth, Cornwall, TR10 9EN, England.

Please enclose a cheque or postal order to the value of the cover price and allow the following for postage and packing:
UK: 80p for the first book, and 20p for each additional book ordered up to a maximum charge of 12.00.
BFPO: 80p for the first book, and 20p for each addition book.
OVERSEAS & EIRE: £1.50 for the first book, £1.00 for the second book, and 30p for each subsequent book.

Name ....

Address ....

....

Postcode ....